The Bishop of Jerusalem

Chuck Thompson

JAMES ONE INSTITUTE

The Bishop of Jerusalem

Published in the U.S. by:
James One Institute
P.O. Box 810
Bristol, TN 37620

Visit James One Institute at
www.jamesoneinstitute.com

Cover design by Christopher Slaughter
Cover image © iStockphoto.com/Vladimir Khirman

ISBN: 978-0-9794116-3-2

"...faith without works is dead."

James 2:26b

To James

Who demonstrated his works with his life,

And his faith with his death.

i

Acknowledgments

To my wife, Barb, and colleagues —Brandon, Craig, and Crystal:
Without your input, talent, and encouragement this novel would
never have existed. Your fingerprints are present throughout its pages.
Thank you.

To my readers—Dan, Joyce, Neil, Matt, and Meredith: Thank you
for allowing me to see through your eyes. Your suggestions are
evident.

To my assistants—Amanda, Bri, Jess, and Lindsey: I don't know
whether to thank you for saving me from the computer or saving the
computer from me.

To the Penheads—Andy, Brandon, Craig, and Tommy: If it were
not for you the first ink would still be in the pen.

To my family—Barb, CJ, Sarah, Erin, Rachel, Matt, Michael, and
Soren: Your love sustains me and your laughter inspires me.

Bless you all.

Introduction

Isn't this the carpenter's son? Isn't his mother's name Mary,
And aren't his brothers James, Joseph, Simon and Jude?
Matthew 13:55

James, the brother of Jesus and writer of the twentieth book of the New Testament was martyred. His death in 62 AD is well documented in historical writings, but his story is not well known.

Tradition tells us the James was the first "Bishop of Jerusalem," however we do not know if the title was used during his time. We do know that the he was the recognized leader of The Way and the Council in Jerusalem. The Jerusalem Council was a group of apostles and elders in Jerusalem. The authority of the Jerusalem Council is documented in Acts 15 and 21 and depicts occasions in which Peter and then Paul return to Jerusalem and give an accounting of their mission activities. In both cases, these patriarchs of Christianity submit to the authority of the Jerusalem Council and in both cases it is the voice of James that represents the Council's discernment.

James' leadership of the early church was not an elected position, but an acknowledgment of an anointing of wisdom. James was not the first leader of the Jerusalem church. Peter was the leader of the Christian church in Jerusalem in the volatile years immediately following Christ's death. The Way, the name the Jerusalem Christians used at that time, was mostly made up of Jews who believed that Jesus was the Messiah. Their number had grown significantly, especially after Pentecost, when the miracle with fire occurred in the Temple courtyard. Many God-fearing people in the Temple Courtyard heard the same words spoken, but each heard it in his native language. This was followed by a time of persecution against the church. The Sadducees were jealous and persecuted the Apostles, yet the church still grew. Soon the persecution against the church got severe enough and the church was scattered from Jerusalem.

The Way enjoyed intermittent periods of calm in Jerusalem, possibly because in Jerusalem the converts were all Jews and still obeyed the rites of circumcision and the customs of Moses, King Herod, who had James the Greater, the brother of John, beheaded, unsettled the calm with his murderous act. James' murder started a spirit of malice amongst the Herodians against the Way. The Herodians were a Jerusalem sect that served their own political interests by serving the interests of the Romans. The Romans expected the Herodians to keep the peace and collect the taxes.

The Herodian persecution of The Way did not stop with Herod's murder of James the Greater, and soon Peter was also arrested. Peter's arrest was too near Passover for Herod to kill him, as he had James, so Herod imprisoned him, avoiding the wrath of the other sects. Surely Peter would have met the same fate as James, but he was freed from his chains by an angel. Peter made his way to Miryam's house, where the other Apostles were congregating. Peter left word with Miryam, her son Mark, and the Apostles that he was leaving Jerusalem. He told them to alert James and his brothers to how the Lord had saved him. In essence, Peter left the leadership of The Way to James. This occurred shortly before the death of Herod Agrippa I in 44 AD. James served as Bishop of Jerusalem until his own death in 62 AD.

The Epistle of James has a curious history. Most casual readers associate the letter with the passage from the second chapter, which says, "Faith without works is dead." This passage prompted Martin Luther to argue that James' Epistle should be removed from the canon. Luther believed that James was promoting a works-based salvation in direct conflict with the saved-by-grace theology of Paul. Luther was not successful in his campaign to eliminate James, but the legacy of his argument persists today.

Another noteworthy reformer, John Calvin, saw no conflict between the theology of James and the theology of Paul. Calvin, however, must have recognized the tension between them, because he defends their harmony in his commentaries.

An emphasis on translating faith into works does not negate faith, nor does it elevate works to the status of the "gate unto salvation." Anyone who could accuse James of minimizing or misunderstanding the price Christ paid for our salvation could not know James' story. James was asked to clearly name the "gate unto salvation" and his answer was not "works." How James answered this question and what his answer cost him is a compelling reason to tell James' story.

The Epistle of James also has a curious writing style. It is very short. Nine short treatises make up the final four chapters. Any one of these nine treatises might have received multiple chapters from another writer. No one would consider James verbose. The most curious chapter is chapter one, which makes the other four look longwinded. In chapter one, James covers a plethora of topics, any one of which could be the focus of a twenty-first century spiritual formation or applied theology book. But for James, twenty-seven verses are enough. Or maybe twenty-seven verses were all he had time to write.

In chapter one, James writes emotionally. Ideas are presented more like an explosion than a philosophical argument, as if James is in a hurry to get everything that he has to say on paper. He moves from one idea to another the way a hurried parent would list nuggets of wisdom to a child the first time he stayed home alone. The last days in James' life may provide an explanation for the urgency in his writing.

The Bishop of Jerusalem is a historical novel based on accounts of the death of James in Jerusalem in 62 AD. Historically, the religious and cultural atmosphere in Jerusalem in 62 AD was steeped in political tension. Each of the seven sects of Judaism, of which Christianity or The Way was one, vied for political advantage and the loyalty of the

Jewish people. From the Book of Acts, and Josephus and Hegesippus, historians from the First and Second Centuries, respectively, we know that for the last several years of his life, James was the Bishop of Jerusalem, the head of The Way. Herod Agrippa II was the King of Israel, and leader of the Herodian sect. Porcius Festus, whose death preceded James', was the Roman Procurator in Jerusalem. Ananus, the Sadducee, was the High Priest at the time of James' death. The Sadducees, the descendants of Levi made up the priestly elite, another of the seven sects. The remaining four sects include two groups of Pharisees, Hillel and Shemmi, the Essenes, a faction from the tribe of Levi that believed the Sadducees had become defiled, and the Zealots, who militantly opposed any form of Roman occupation of Israel.

The Bishop of Jerusalem speculates about how these real historical figures and sects related to one another and shaped the historical events that preceded James' martyrdom. *The Bishop of Jerusalem* offers a possible explanation of why James may have written that first chapter, why he wrote it in such a hurried manner, and how the Holy Spirit might have used the trials in James' life to inspire his epistle.

CHAPTER ONE

James, a servant of God
James 1:1a

W ho do you think you are?" She yelled as she stood and leaned against the table between her and James. She did not notice her shawl falling from her lap. The display of anger shocked the young Rabbi Symeon who lurched forward from his seat on the opposite side of the room where he sat with two elders from his synagogue. "Mind yourself, woman. This man is the brother of the Messiah," he said as he pointed at James without noticing James' head flinch back as he spoke, "You will mind your tongue towards him or you will have to explain yourself to the elders." The sternness in his voice matched the glare in his eyes.

Symeon was an average-sized man who would probably go unnoticed on the streets of Jerusalem except for his bright red hair and beard. His red features amplified the outrage that had risen within him. It had only been a year ago that Symeon had been appointed the Rabbi of Bezetha, the newest synagogue in Jerusalem. At twenty-five, he was the youngest Rabbi to receive his own synagogue. The Bezetha synagogue, like most Jerusalem synagogues, met in the home of its Rabbi. Rabbi Symeon's home was on the eastern edge of the Bezetha section of Jerusalem. Since his installation as Rabbi of Bezetha, this was the first time Symeon had asked the Jerusalem Council for help. Symeon seemed surprised and a bit nervous that James, the Bishop of Jerusalem himself, had been the one to come. A woman feeling the freedom for such boldness could be seen as an indication of a young Rabbi's lack of control over his flock.

Turning to face James, Symeon's voice slowed and deepened, "I am sorry, your excellence. She is a simple woman under a great strain. Please bear her this indiscretion."

James sighed. She had asked a good question: "Who do you think you are?" Why should this woman who sat before him know who he was? She appeared to be in her middle years, but her skin, especially her hands, seemed weathered beyond her age. Her voice sounded angry, but she looked to James to be more fearful than angry. To her, he probably seemed like just another man she was expected to answer to.

He knew that he had touched a wound in her, but he did not know why asking her how she had come to Jerusalem could prompt such a strong reaction. He would have preferred to have been left alone to respond to her question, but that had not happened. She needed a gentle hand, but instead she had received a strong authoritative rebuke. And to make matters even more offensive to James the rebuke had invoked his status as the brother of Messiah.

He was the Bishop of Jerusalem and the brother of the Messiah, but those titles had become ways people expressed what they expected him to do. He was fifty-one years old, but it still made him wince when people attempted to force their expectations on him, especially when their expectations were to use his titles to guilt, scold, or manipulate others into submission. Being the brother of the Messiah was difficult enough without well-meaning Rabbis using it for their own agenda.

Noticing how people thought and what they did during trials came naturally to him. It was part of his calling to minister to people in times of struggle. Often in the role of Rabbi, he was called upon to exhort and confront. Holding the role of Bishop added that much more strength to his exhortation, but it was guidance that he preferred. And it was clear to James that this woman of Bezetha was not in need of exhortation. It was not defiance or lack of instruction that defined her now, but woundedness. Rather than the direct approach of an authority, she needed the more gentle hand of a guide and the young Rabbi and his two elders, who sat along the wall with watchful eyes and their sense of propriety, were interfering with his calling. He wanted to ask one of them, "Who do *you* think I am?" But he would not do that, not today anyway.

There was no reason to ask the question because the answer would be inevitable, "You are the brother of the Messiah."

James picked up the shawl from the floor, and as he faced the irritated woman he said, "I fear that I have offended you. It is not what I intended, and I ask that you bear me this indiscretion."

It was not lost on the elders that James had chosen to use Symeon's words of apology. Symeon lowered his shoulders and settled back against the wall. The other two men followed suit. James wanted to be left to himself as he ministered to this woman, but getting the elders to leave them alone would require diplomacy, lest he offend them as well. How could this woman feel comfortable enough to receive guidance from him if she thought that he was a judge over her? How could she have thought otherwise with a panel of elders sitting on one side of the room, with their arms folded, and watching her every movement. *She must think that a Sanhedrin tribunal has been convened,* thought James.

The angry woman leaned forward and placed her hands on the edge of the rough wooden table that stood between her and James. Her eyes were still wide open as she studied James' face.

He handed her the shawl. "I would very much like to start over if that would please you," James said in a soft voice.

She nodded slightly without speaking and took the shawl from him. "Thank you."

"It is a lovely shawl. I don't think that I have ever seen one like it."

3

"Thank you," she said again.

"I noticed flecks of something shining in the fabric. I have never seen fabric like that before."

"It was a wedding gift from my mother-in-law. She was a weaver and made it herself."

"And how did she get the shiny flecks into the fabric?" James asked.

"It was her own idea," she said, seemingly more eager to speak. "She found a certain kind of river rock that she could crush and imbed into fabric with a mixture of sycamore sap and water." She sat back and added, "I don't know what kind of rock it was."

"I would have guessed that the sycamore sap would have stained the fabric," observed James.

"It does stain, sir. You are right." She held the shawl up again, "That is why it is only on the darker corners."

"I see. I thought that it was unusual for a shawl to be so dark, but that explains it. It is very lovely. It must be of great value to you." Then, with his right hand over his heart, he said, "My name is James, by the way."

She seemed confused. He had said exactly the same thing earlier.

James moved his hand from his chest and gestured at her. "And you are Mary as I remember it."

Mary nodded in agreement.

"I like the name Mary. My mother's name was Mary, too."

"I knew that sir," Mary said meekly.

James nodded and reminded himself again that most people already knew his family. "I do not mean to alarm you again, Mary, but I could not help but notice that you reacted very strongly to what I thought was a simple question." He could see Mary's shoulders tense, so he held both his hands out towards her, "I now know that it was not a simple question, but I want you to know that I did not know that then."

He could see her shoulders relax again. "I just want you to know that I did not come here to upset you, Mary."

She stared at him, and then slowly turned her eyes towards the three elders along the wall.

James had hoped to avoid asking the elders to leave, as he believed that he had already embarrassed them, but it was not to be avoided. "Brothers, might I beg of you to leave Mary and me to this business by ourselves?"

The two elders looked to Symeon for a response. Symeon looked back at them and, leaning forward, said, "As you wish, Bishop." After a moment of hesitation he added, "What of propriety, my lord? No one would dare suspect you of an impropriety, but she is an unmarried woman. Your reputation must be protected."

"My reputation, such as it is, should never get in the way of the work that the Lord has appointed me to do." James could hear that his tone was gruffer than he intended, so he softened his voice. "But, for propriety's sake, leave brother Myron here with us until you can send another woman from your flock back." *To guard us against the judgment of wolves*, he thought.

Myron looked helpless as he watched the other two men leave the room. As they left, James studied the room. It was the front room of Rabbi Symeon's home, where the Bezetha synagogue met. James had understood that there were twenty-four members, but he could not picture them all in a room this small. Besides the simple wooden table and two chairs occupied by him and Mary, there were two backless benches along the adjacent walls to the left behind James' chair. A large arched doorway leading to the rest of Symeon's home was on his right. James assumed that the arched doorway led to the area where the women would gather during worship and prayers. Across from where James sat and behind Mary was a door to the street with windows on either side of it. The rough wooden door and shudders matched the rough wooden style of the furniture in the room. The quality of the

5

woodworking was sturdy enough, but insufficient to be acceptable in any other section of Jerusalem. Bezetha was the poorest section in many ways.

James turned his attention to Mary. She still had her attention focused on Symeon who was closing a woven curtain across the arched doorway. When the curtain finally closed, she turned her face towards James.

"Would you care to hear what I was told about you before I came here to meet you?" James asked.

"Yes sir."

"Rabbi Symeon sent word to the Jerusalem Council that there was a woman in his flock that he was worried about. I assume he meant you."

Mary raised one eyebrow. "Worried?"

"'Concerned' was the exact word that I heard, but I did not speak directly to him myself."

Mary still looked confused.

"Symeon came to the Jerusalem synagogue and spoke to one of the other Rabbis there. I believe that it was Bemus. Bemus is who I talked to."

Mary tipped her head to the left.

"Bemus was going to come himself, but I said that I preferred to do it."

"Sir."

"Yes, Mary?"

"What were you told about...me?"

James hesitated before he answered. He generally answered direct questions honestly, believing that people deserved to be told the truth. But he knew that people were not always ready to receive every truth. He chose his words carefully, "I believe that the exact phrase was that the concern for you was over a relationship you have with a Roman soldier."

6

Mary flinched.

"Do you have a relationship with a Roman soldier?"

Mary looked down. "I do have a friend. A male friend. His name is Marcus." Looking up she added, "He is a Roman soldier."

James held eye contact with her and watched as her eyes searched his face.

"There is nothing wrong with our relationship," she said with resolve.

James smiled slightly.

"He brings me food and a few coins, and I do his mending and the mending of his friends. He is generous and treats me more like a mother than anything else." She stood and leaned across the table, "I swear that it is nothing else."

"Mary." James opened his hands, "I am not accusing you of anything."

Mary looked at Myron who was staring at James, then through squinted eyes looked back at James.

"I am not accusing you of anything," he repeated.

She stood slowly and then sat back down, holding to a rather stiff posture.

"Has someone else accused you, Mary?"

Mary relaxed slightly but rolled her eyes.

Laughing gently, James offered, "I know what it is like to be accused of something based simply upon circumstances." He was going to tell her a story about being accused by a Sadducee of betraying his Jewish heritage because of his profession of the Messiah, but she did not give him the opportunity.

"Do you know what it is like to be an unmarried woman?" she asked.

He assumed that it was a rhetorical question, but when it appeared that she was waiting for an answer, he admitted, "No, I do not know what it is like to be an unmarried woman."

Mary moved to the edge of her seat and began speaking in a softer voice. Her face looked more animated, and she seemed less conscious of the watchful Myron along the wall. From experience, James knew this meant Mary was more comfortable.

James found spiritual guidance more rewarding than preaching. When preaching, he told his flock, "Here is the truth, go and discern for yourselves how and when to apply it." With an individual, he was required to be much more involved with the hows and whens of applying the truth to a particular life. Much of the truth that he preached to groups was learned from conversations with someone enduring a trial.

Mary started to speak. "We hear the Rabbis talk about freedom and equality all the time at the synagogue. It all sounds good when you hear it. But for an unmarried woman, it can sound like nothing more than an empty promise that one would tell a child to keep her from asking questions." She leaned back but kept her hands on the table. "I cherish the hope that one day I will be resurrected and made whole, but what of today? What about now?" She spread her hands out and gestured around the room. "I attend worship. I attend prayers. But what about me? Am I a leper?"

"What are you saying Mary? Are you being mistreated by the synagogue?"

She turned red and her shoulders slumped. "No, no one is mistreating me."

"Are you in need of food or other provisions?"

"No. I mean yes I am in need of that kind of help, but The Way in Jerusalem, even in Bezetha, is well known for their distribution of food. I am well cared for that way."

"In what way are you not being cared for, Mary?"

She looked at James as if she were asking 'do you really want to know?' and finally confessed, "No one...talks to me."

"No one?"

8

"Marcus talks to me."

"Is Marcus one of the brethren?"

"He is not, at least not yet. But he is curious, and he asks me questions. I think that I could ask him to synagogue if it were not for the loose tongues of fish wives."

The harshness of the term "fish wives" caught James' attention, but before he could mention it, the curtain across the arched doorway open and a woman peered in.

The woman stepped into the room without displacing the curtain. Her pointed nose and thin lips gave her a mouse-like appearance, and the manner in which her eyes darted around the room added to the picture.

"Excuse me, sir," she said, "Rabbi Symeon told me to join you."

James stood and motioned towards the bench where Myron was already leaving, "Yes sister, please come in and join us." Escorting Myron to the front door, the two men nodded to one another, and James excused him with a hand on his shoulder. Then, turning towards the nervous woman on the bench, he smiled and said, "Thank you for joining us. I am James and this is Mary."

The woman glanced at Mary, tipped her head, and then returned her gaze to James. She said nothing.

"Are you a member of this synagogue?"

She clinched her teeth awkwardly, took a deep breath, and announced, "I am the Rabbi's wife, I mean I am Rabbi Symeon's wife." She pointed at the door, "He said that you needed me to be here."

"Yes sister, we do. I hope that it is not too much of a disruption to your day."

She smiled.

"What would you like us to call you?" James asked.

"Oh, I'm sorry." She placed her hand upon her chest just below the nape of her neck. "I am Isaura."

"May God, our Father, bless you for this offering of your time, Isaura."

Isaura squirmed on the bench.

"Isaura, do you know Mary?"

Looking toward Mary, Isaura slowly bowed her head. "Yes, we see each other at worship and prayers."

"I have come to Bezetha to offer spiritual direction to your sister Mary, and we need your presence and support as a witness. Is that acceptable to you?"

Isaura nodded her acceptance.

"Thank you, Isaura."

As he turned to Mary, James could not help but wonder about the relationship between those two women. He wondered if Mary considered Isaura to be a loose-tongued fishwife.

"The question that I asked you earlier, the one that upset you so much—" James hesitated to discern if Mary was listening or reacting to him before continuing— "I do not understand why it upset you. I do not want to upset you again with the same question, but I do want you to know that I am interested in whatever it is that..." He struggled to find the right word to finish the question.

Mary finished it for him. "You want to know what happened in my life that led me to Jerusalem, don't you?"

"I want to know anything that will help me know and guide you better."

"My husband, Evan, and I lived in Tiberias with our son, Illias. Tiberias is a city on the southwestern side of the Sea of Galilee." She paused, waiting for James to respond.

James leaned forward. "I know the city."

"My husband was a fisherman." She inhaled deeply, "I'm sorry, I thought that I had already cried all my tears." Then the tears began to appear at the corners of her eyes.

James waited patiently for her to continue. He knew that she was touching upon tender memories.

She moved her chair back from the table and turned it slightly so she could see out of the window that had been at her back. Mary's breathing became slow and loud enough for James to hear. "It had been a bad season, a dry season. That makes the fish move deeper and makes it harder for fishermen to earn a living." She stopped speaking and controlled her breathing again before continuing. "On that day, he had been out all day and had made such a nice catch that he decided to go back out again in the evening."

"'Just a short one,' he said, 'while the fish are asking to be caught.' He never went back out without sorting his nets first, but he was in a hurry. It was my suggestion that Illias go with him. I thought that he could help his father with the nets." She stared at nothing out the window, "The last thing he said to me was, 'We'll be back soon after dark with enough fish for a banquet for my queen.'"

James watched her sit staring out the window. He could see tears roll slowly down her right cheek. When she finally wiped her cheek, he asked, "Were those his last words to you?"

She nodded yes without looking back.

The silence was heavy and James knew to wait on her.

Standing abruptly, she wiped her face once more and stated, "I can't do this." She turned to the door to leave but did not step towards it.

"I understand, Mary. It is hard to talk about the things that weigh us down. It is hard, but it is good to talk about them, too."

Mary shrugged.

"Mary, if Isaura would agree to join me, could I come to visit you at your home instead of meeting again here. Would that be acceptable to you?"

Mary nodded and left without looking back.

James looked at Isaura, who was still sitting on the bench, "I hope that I have not misspoken, Isaura. I can ask Symeon to help find another woman from the synagogue if you cannot or would prefer not to go to Mary's home."

Isaura stood up and started to speak, then looked past James.

"Rabbi," came a booming voice from behind him. James turned to see Symeon standing just inside the arched doorway.

"I am so sorry," Symeon said as he approached James, "she is in need of exhortation, and I will see to it swiftly."

"Rabbi," James said, "she meant me no offense and I took no offense."

"That is not the point. You are being too gracious."

"Excuse me," James said curtly, aware that he could easily become angry.

"You cannot let her treat authority with disrespect. She cannot submit to God her Father, who she cannot see, if she does not submit to authority that she can see."

Slow down, James told himself. This was precisely the kind of religiosity that found intolerable. "Rabbi Symeon, I appreciate your zeal, but I would appreciate it if you would let me address the manner in which Mary has treated me."

"But Bishop . . ."

"Rabbi, I prefer that you leave this for me. I believe that her question of who I am was what the Lord wanted me to hear."

"Who you are?" Symeon repeated, looking confused.

"Yes, who I am. It is a good question to ask ourselves from time to time. And I believe that the Lord might be telling me that it is my time." James turned and smiled at Isaura. "At least it is time for me to make my leave, Isaura, thank you for helping me. If I come back tomorrow, would you go with me to Mary's home?"

Isaura looked at her husband and then back at James before saying, "Certainly."

Turning to Symeon James said, "I will return tomorrow. May God bless and keep you. And now, I must go." James walked to the door.

"Do you have an answer?" Symeon asked.

"An answer?"

"To whom you think you are?"

"I do."

CHAPTER TWO

James, a servant of...the Lord Jesus the Messiah
James 1:1b

James was relieved to be outside again. He would be home in half an hour if no one stopped him as he crossed Jerusalem. The sky was unusually dark for early evening. An early dark sky always meant a cold wind was coming. Sometimes a cold wind meant rain. As he began his walk west through Bezetha towards the Fish Gate in the old city walls, he tugged at the shawl around his shoulders. Tugging at his shawl reassured him that the shawl was around his neck if he needed it. The gesture also reassured him that he was headed home.

Symeon's home was along the northeast border of Bezetha. Just inside the wall Herod Agrippa I constructed fifteen years earlier, Bezetha sat, lower than the rest of the city. That meant that James would be walking uphill until he reached the Fish Gate. He dreaded the possibility of rain coming before he reached the North Wall because rain on top of the dusty roads of Bezetha would make the hill beneath the Fish Gate slippery. The thought of falling quickened his step; slippery was too much strain for his tired old knees. The other option was to walk around to the Sheep Gate, which was all the way at the southern end of the North Wall.

As James walked, he stopped noticing any of the stone dwellings that he passed. He paid just enough attention to his surroundings to avoid tripping over the loose stones that spotted the walkways and to nod a greeting to anyone who passed him by. For years he had heard complaints that he had passed this person or that person on the street and had failed to greet them properly. Social niceties were not his strength, but he had not yet felt convicted enough about it to change. He liked to let his thoughts drift as he walked the familiar streets to his home.

His thoughts drifted to Mary. He knew that Mary's angry outburst was something of importance. She angered quickly, but she was not being disrespectful, of that he was sure. He had accidentally stumbled on to a wounded part of her soul, and she had reacted as if he had pricked her flesh, reopening the wound. He bore her no ill will for her words or for leaving Symeon's home so abruptly.

If he bore ill will at anyone, it would be this young Rabbi and his elders who seemed to have their expectations of him. He had thought about asking Symeon, "Who do *you* think I am?" when the young Rabbi scolded Mary for asking the same. The three men had apologized profusely after Mary had left them. It was as if they were embarrassed by how she, a woman, had treated a man of James' rank. As if they expected her primary response to his ministry to be reverence or fear of his rank.

James had held his own tongue when the Elders of Bezetha had implied that James had been "too gracious" with her. "Too gracious!" The words from their lips suggested weakness. "Her disrespect must be addressed," they had said. He felt his anger rising again as he remembered their unsolicited advice. Unsolicited advice always irritated him. It only made his irritation worse when that advice was off of the mark, as theirs was.

James was confident that he could recognize and confront disrespect for the authority of his office. He was the Bishop of Jerusalem, and if it fell upon him, as it often did, to make a decision that affected all of the brethren, he could do it. And he could do so with the full authority of his office. Yet, his authority as Bishop of

Jerusalem had never been questioned or disrespected. He carried himself with such confidence that a challenge to his authority as inconceivable.

James knew that some thought of him as arrogant because of this confidence, but he worried little about them. His confidence was not based upon pride in his wisdom, his knowledge, or his ability. James' confidence was based upon his assurance in his call.

James had not asked to be Bishop, nor had he wanted to be Bishop. He would have chosen something else for himself. Perhaps he could have continued his training to be a carpenter like his father. His son was a carpenter. His brother had been a carpenter, for a while. As he thought of his brother as a carpenter his mind wandered.

James was somewhat startled to realize that his feet were not moving and that he was no longer walking. How long had his thoughts drifted so far away in the reflection of the past? When he lifted his eyes to get a bearing on where he was, he smiled to see that he had stopped in front of an open shelter where a carpenter was working on a table with a young man. James watched them work for a moment. The young man studied the older carpenter as he attached the last leg of a table. James imagined that the younger man was wishing he could be doing the work himself. It was a tender memory for James, and he could almost hear his father say, "Patience, my son. Your time will come and when it is your time to build, you will build things to last." "Patience, son," James said under his breath.

He smiled contently, and then remembered that he was racing the rain and quickened his pace once again. The sky had grown even darker and the air had indeed become chilly, but he had not felt a drop of rain yet. He could see the cleft in the North Wall that marked the Fish Gate, but the gate itself would not come into view until he turned left at the top of the hill he was just beginning to climb. He turned his thoughts to home. His wife, Bat-Ami, would be preparing their evening meal, and he smiled as he wondered if she would try to hide

16

parsnip roots in something that she fed him. He did not really dislike parsnip roots as much as he liked the little game they played. Games like this let him be human. She let him be human. It was not just the warmth of her home, her meal, or her smile that he looked forward to on such cold walks back home. What he treasured most was the freedom that she gave him. She expected a lot of her husband, and she was not shy about saying so when her expectations were not met. But she never expected him to be anyone other than who he was.

As a public figure, James knew that everyone associated with him expected something. Within the last week he had been asked by a frustrated father to scare a sense of responsibility into his youthful son, and to recommend another young man as a potential husband for a woman whose parents wanted her to marry a rabbi. The original converts from Peter expected him to preach sermons about the fulfillment of the Torah while the more recent converts to The Way expected sermons from the hillside teachings of Jesus. James had made peace with most of the expectations of people; he pleased some and disappointed others. He was determined that he would never surrender his call or his responsibility to capricious expectations. But he also wanted to make sure that he at least listened to the expectations of people. His Hillel school Rabbi had often said, "The Lord our God often gives us wisdom through the trials of others."

His meandering thoughts stopped suddenly as he stubbed his toe on a rock in the street. He grimaced silently and knelt down to massage his wound. As he began walking again, more slowly now, his thoughts drifted back to the scene in Symeon's house where he had felt the disapproval of the Bezetha Elders for being too soft and permissive in response to what they considered the disrespect of a woman.

In anger, James imagined himself saying, "Your disrespect for my judgment is more infuriating than her cries of pain. How dare you hint that I need your intercession? Where were you when Paul sought my spiritual direction when he returned to Jerusalem? Paul submitted to my authority when he returned from Caesarea fearing the rumors of his crimes against the Torah. I had no trouble confronting Paul himself and sending him to the Temple to go through the rites of purification."

A large single drop of rain hit the top of James' head. It made him realize that he had stopped again. He looked around and was startled to find the Fish Gate was on his right. It would have been on his left had he just walked to the top of the hill and turned. But he had stopped at the top of the hill and turned completely around as if to preach at Symeon's house from across Bezetha. The thought caused him to flush with embarrassment, as did his quickness to assume that Symeon had expected him to be harsher. Jumping to partially true conclusions was a familiar error on his part, and it was why he had trained himself to hold his tongue when he felt angry.

Another drop of cold rain fell on his head, cooling him and his embarrassment. He realized Symeon's age. The young Rabbi was respectful every time they had interacted before. Symeon had been commissioned to his own synagogue over a year ago, and since that time he had attended James' synagogue at least once a month, Temple at least once a week, and quite regularly the council meetings. There was no basis for James to assume that Symeon's comments were anything other than misguided embarrassment.

"Shalom, Rabbi."

"Shalom," returned James, although he did not recognize the young man who had greeted him.

The raindrops started coming in greater numbers so James refitted his shawl to cover his head. He was only half way home, but the streets were better in the old city to the north of the Temple, and they were flatter, too. It still might take as long as the walk through Bezetha because the chance of meeting people who would want to stop and talk would be much greater around the Temple.

With his head covered, James did not notice that the rain increased, or that the number of people on the streets had decreased. His mind had drifted once again to Mary's question, "Who do you think you are?"

I am the Bishop of Jerusalem, he thought sarcastically, because being the Head of the Jerusalem Council would not have been what James would have chosen for his life if the choosing was his to do.

There were reasons why James was the Bishop of Jerusalem, but none of them because he wanted to be the Bishop. Being Bishop of Jerusalem, the Head of the Jerusalem Council, was an honor, but a bittersweet honor. It placed great pressure on his young family, and they all received far more attention and scrutiny than any of them wanted. His wife Bat-Ami and their two sons Nicholas and Leander were all proud of him and of the work he did, but they were, too often, functionally a widow and orphans.

The pressure on James was great, too. He settled theological disputes between Peter and Paul, he made the final decisions about the conversion of the Gentiles, he led the Jerusalem synagogue, and he managed the political struggle with the other six sects vying for political leverage and position in Jerusalem. These were the pressures of his life, and he managed them well because of his unflinching confidence in his calling to the position. The pressure he failed to manage well was from many well-intentioned people whose assumptions about who he was were wrong.

These people expected that anyone who had seen Jesus would have looked into His eyes and known that He was the Messiah. These people assumed that they would have known and believed. Their faith was strong enough now that they would give their lives for Jesus. They could not remember not believing, nor could they imagine that though he had grown up with Jesus as his brother every day of his life, he had not known that his brother was the Lord until after Jesus had been crucified and resurrected. When Jesus was in the Jordan with the Baptist, James was at Hillel school. While Jesus was teaching on the hillsides, James was studying the Torah. James had been at the wedding in Canaan, but he had not drunk the wine because he had been set apart from birth, neither drinking wine nor cutting his hair.

Not recognizing Jesus as the Messiah during Jesus' time in the world was a sorrow that plagued James from a quiet place deep within his heart. Even when the crowds followed Jesus and reported miracles, James had not believed. He and his younger brother Jude had stood in the back of a synagogue once and listened to Jesus teach, and He was a wonderful teacher, but they feared for their older brother's safety as he attracted the Pharisees' resentment. Jude had not recognized Jesus either, but they both loved Him. They loved the Messiah like a brother, and they feared for Him like brothers would. How could James expect anyone else to understand what that was like?

No one who knew James doubted his love of God, his devotion to the Torah, or his observance of the traditions. That was one of the ways that he had been prepared for being Bishop long before he became Bishop. But his devotion to the Messiah was confusing; the Messiah was, after all, also his brother. His devotion to the Messiah was complete, but it was not what people expected and their expectations reminded him that he had let his brother down. And not just his brother; he had let his mother down as well.

He swallowed hard and quickened his pace in a vain attempt to keep the thoughts and memories from coming. But it was no use; the scene came back to him as if he had seen it himself. He could see her in his mind's eye: Mary, standing at the foot of the cross, being held by John, and watching her son, James' brother, die horribly. And where was James?

James swallowed hard again and deliberately deepened his breathing. He was home. How could he be home when his innocent brother, the Messiah, was being arrested, betrayed, mocked, and murdered? How could he be home? He was studying the Torah, but he should have gone to Jerusalem with his mother. It was Passover. Not going to Jerusalem for Passover was an egregious decision. He should have gone, but he did not go. He did not accompany his mother, which was his duty as the oldest male at home. He could not begrudge Joseph's absence, but Jesus had been gone for over three years, and in spite of what he knew now, he wondered, *Could I really have resented Jesus' absence?*

James took note of his surroundings, hoping that no one was watching him. Thankfully he had the street to himself. *I should have been with my family. Why did I resent Jesus' absence so much? Why did I not just do what I knew was right to do? It was the moment when Jesus needed me most...and I was home...pouting. It was the moment mother needed me most...and I was home...teaching her a lesson she had no need to learn.*

He wiped moisture from the corner of his right eye with the back of his hand. He remembered a woman that had been a member of The Way. Her name was Priscilla and she had been widowed for three years when she asked James to visit her and her son, Joel. Joel was not her oldest son but the oldest son still living with her and she had wanted James, as Bishop, to impress upon the young man his duty. "The Bishop would never let his mother go to Temple alone," she had said. "He is the brother of the Lord."

Priscilla was no longer living, but the shame her words brought still stung. He had felt used, exposed, and ashamed. All he could think to do was put everything he felt to the side and tend to Priscilla and her son. And to the side it went where it joined alongside all of the other memories and encounters that reminded him that he was not now, nor would he ever be, what people would expect from the brother of the Messiah.

He made himself turn away and begin walking towards his home again. A tender recognition came. *My mother never burdened me with the accusation that I should have known. It would have been her right to do so,* he thought as he pictured Mary collapsing in John's arms as

Jesus told her, "This is your son." *John is your son, Mother, because your other son was not there.*

John had taken Mary to his home after Jesus was crucified. James and Jude had joined her there shortly after. That was the place and time that they began to understand what they had missed for so long. In many ways John had become older brother to he and Jude as well as Mary's son. It was John who nurtured their young faith and told them of the three missing years with their brother. *I should have been there with you, Mother.*

As James reached the corner where he would turn to go home, he looked back at the Temple before it disappeared behind the rest of the city. Sometimes when his memory would slip into this familiar dark hole, it would help to remind himself of what he knew to be right. He was the Bishop of Jerusalem and he had work to do, work he had been equipped for and called to do. It was his to do, his to obey, whether or not he had regrets that haunted him.

James whispered out loud, "I am sorry. I should have been there for you at the end." This time the picture in James' mind was not of Mary, but of Jesus.

James let tears run down his cheeks as he noticed he was standing in front of his own home. When he finally realized he was home, he managed to return his thoughts to the day. When he remembered Mary's question he thought, *I wish I had said that I am "James, a servant of Jesus the Messiah."*

CHAPTER THREE

...to the Twelve Tribes disbursed among the nations.
James 1:1c

Bat-Ami stood waiting for her husband inside the front window. She and James had been friends since childhood, and their marriage of thirty-plus years was built on their friendship. She knew that theirs was an unusual marriage. Most Jerusalem wives had to mind their tongues much more than she. She was careful not to exercise her freedom in public settings, but that was a concession to the condition of other women rather than a requirement of her husband. She did not want her freedom to make other wives feel badly or to encourage them to take dangerous risks asserting themselves.

Jude was the first member of James' family that Bat-Ami had come to know. They were both children, but only Jude, the boy, was being taught to read and write. She was not allowed to read and write, but she wanted to learn, and Jude, who struggled with his studies, wanted at least one person in his life to be less skillful than he was, so Jude taught Bat to read. Their arrangement continued for nearly a year before Jude's mother, Mary discovered it. Mary had noticed that her son's reading had improved at an unexpected and unexplained pace, which made her curious. When she began to inquire about it, she discovered that Jude's education was benefiting from his instruction of Bat-Ami. Mary approved, maybe because she herself desired the skill of letters and did not understand why it should be denied her, but Joseph's objection made sense to her as well. Joseph was concerned about how Bat-Ami might be treated by others if it were known that she had done the forbidden. It was James, even though he was only twelve years old at the time, who settled the impasse. James said that the teaching of women did not violate the Torah, but only the tradition of the fathers, which should be respected but not obeyed as if it had the same authority as the Torah. James said that Bat-Ami's instruction should continue as it brought blessing to two, not just one, but that she should be carefully instructed in the use and open display of her blessing. James' older brother, Jesus, had been completely silent throughout the entire discussion, but when it was over He had said "Well done" to His younger brother. That was the moment that Bat-Ami realized that she loved James, and that had not changed ever since.

James and Bat-Ami had spent nearly three decades in this home together, raising their two sons into adulthood. Leander, the eldest son, had, since he was of age, apprenticed with Alfonse, a carpenter who lived and worked beyond the Essene gate on the eastern outskirts of Jerusalem. Alfonse had learned his craft in Florence, Italy, and after his wife died, he moved back to Israel, to be close to the Temple. For the past eight years, Leander lived and worked and worshipped alongside of the old man. Leander had become so much like a son to him that six months ago when Alfonse died of old age, he bequeathed his home and all of his worldly possessions to the young man he had said "helped him live well and die peacefully."

Nicholas, the younger son, had trained to be a Rabbi and was in residence at his first appointment at a synagogue in Lydda. It would have been natural for the son of the Bishop to have received an appointment in Jerusalem where he could also be in service to the Jerusalem Council, but Nicholas would not hear of it. James had been disappointed to see his son leave, but he was also proud of his youngest son's conviction.

After hearing James at their door, Bat-Ami opened the door and questioned him, "James the slave? Is this my husband? Is this James the Just, James of the Calloused Knees, the Bishop of Jerusalem?" These were all names that her husband had come to be known by.

Stepping through their door, James removed his shawl and placed it on a bench near the door. "Is that how you speak of me when I am gone, Bat-Ami?" he asked as he kissed her on the cheek. She was not

24

quite as tall as he, and she did not possess a particularly feminine body, but she was strong and healthy, and he found her to be the most beautiful of women.

Bat-Ami stood quietly, arms folded, and watched her husband turn from her and run his fingers over the *mezuzah* nailed to their door. She waited while he prayed the *shma*, a ritual commanded in Deuteronomy and devoutly obeyed by her husband and his family.

She listened as he recited the words out loud, "Hear, O Israel: The Lord our God, the Lord is one. Love the Lord your God with all your heart, and with all your soul, and with all your strength."

After he opened his eyes and closed their door, Bat-Ami unfolded her arms and pointed to his shawl on the bench. "To me you are my husband who, like a child, cannot find the peg for his shawl."

She picked up his shawl and rolled her eyes. "This shawl is wet." Holding it out towards James she asked, "Do you know what happens to a wet shawl when it is wadded up on a bench?"

He took the shawl from her hand and held it like he was weighing it. "It rots," he finally answered sheepishly.

"Yes, Master Bishop," she said with an undisguised edge to her voice. "A wet shawl rots when it is wadded up on a bench." She turned from him and walked towards the back of their home. "I kept the soup hot for you."

James and Bat-Ami ate their meals at a simple table. James ran his hand across the surface of the table and compared its smoothness to the rough finished table where he had sat that afternoon. Dinner was soup and flatbread. Bat-Ami had prepared it in the room where they were sitting and cooked it on an outside terrace behind their home. She served their food, and when she sat James offered a blessing. Their evening conversation, as usual, started on the events of the day.

"How was your day?" she asked, "You went out to Bezetha, didn't you?"

"I did," James answered as he tore off a small piece of the flatbread from the platter in the center of the table. "It was a difficult day for everyone, I think. The Rabbi from Bezetha came to the synagogue and told us that he was concerned about a woman in his flock." He put the bread in his mouth. "I think that he wanted me to scare her. Instead of scaring her I upset her."

"That does not sound like you."

"I certainly did not mean to upset her. I asked her about how she came to Jerusalem, and she erupted with anger."

Bat-Ami narrowed her eyes. "Why would she get angry with you for asking that?"

"Something about my question must have been too close to something painful for her."

Bat-Ami relaxed and smiled at her husband.

"I wish I had not asked the question."

"James! How could you have known that it would bother her so?"

"I know that I could not have known that, Bat. But I should have known that there was some kind of trial going on in her life."

"Do you know what trial she is facing, James?" Bat-Ami asked as she picked up her spoon and began eating her soup.

"It may have something to do with the deaths of her husband and her son."

"Oh my, James," she said with a solemn look upon her face, "that poor woman. For anyone to have to go through that twice—" she shook her head— "I cannot imagine . . ."

"She did not go through it twice, Bat. She lost them both at the same time."

Placing her spoon back on the table she asked, "What happened?"

"She did not share much, and today was not the time for me to ask questions, but what she told me was that her husband was a fisherman and that the last time she saw either of them was when he took their son out on the lake to seek a second catch for the day."

"He was going out to fish for a second time. Was he a greedy man?"

James shook his head. "I do not think that it was greed that drove him to go back out. She said that it had been dry and the fishing had not been good."

"Oh," said Bat-Ami as she nodded.

"In fact," James said as he turned his left hand over, "their last conversation before he left to go fish was blessing."

"What did they say?"

"He told her that he was going to set before her a banquet for his queen."

"Those were his last words?"

"That is what she told me," answered James.

James noticed that Bat-Ami tilted her head slightly to the right. "What are you thinking, Bat?"

She looked down. "I wondered if she thought of that conversation as a blessing."

"I do not think that she remembers it as a blessing," James explained. "Not yet, anyway. But there will come a time when knowing that he thought of her as his queen will be a source of comfort to her."

"For her sake, James, I pray that you are right. Did you tell her that you thought that it was a blessing?"

James nodded no, "I did not see the value in saying it. Hopefully she will come to see that for herself."

For a few minutes they ate their soup in silence.

"Do you like the soup?" Bat-Ami asked.

"I do," James answered without looking up. He filled his spoon and asked, "What is it?"

Bat-Ami sat silently and waited for James to notice that she was not answering his question.

James looked up. "Why are you smiling, Bat?" Then looking at his bowl he continued, "What is in the soup, Bat? Parsnips!"

"Carrots and thyme and bay leaves."

"It's good. I can taste the thyme." He tore off a scrap of flatbread and scooped up a chunk of carrot from his bowl.

"And parsnips," she said, almost inaudibly.

"Parsnips!" He sighed. "I knew it! Why do you torment me so?"

She shook her head. "You liked the soup not more than a minute ago. Why do you torment me so?"

"You cannot expect me to like it now that I know the deception with which it was made." As he finished the last two spoonfuls in his bowl, he said, "You surely don't expect me to eat it now, do you?"

"I have been your wife a long time, James."

"And?"

"And I have come to expect the unexpected from life with you."

James held out his empty bowl. "And I have come to expect the unexpected in my dinner."

Smiling to herself, Bat-Ami stood up and removed the soup bowls and what was left of the flatbread from the table. She returned to the table and, standing next to him, handed him the last piece of flatbread. She stroked his cheek with the back of her hand. "Is there anything else bothering you, James? Anything else about your trip to Bezetha?"

Leaning his body towards her hand James softly said, "I thought...no, I hoped that I was going to minister to this woman."

"Are you well?" she asked as she felt his forehead.

"I'm fine. I'm just tired."

Bat-Ami took a step back from him and looked at him in a manner that meant she expected him to say more. Sitting back down, she reached across the table and placed her hand on top of his hand, which was resting on their table.

"I am sorry to burden you with these things, Bat. You do not need my struggles."

She squeezed his hand. "You are not burdening me with your struggles. You are letting me into your life. It is where I belong. Now tell me, what did the people in Bezetha expect you to do?"

"I am not entirely sure, but I suspect that the fiery young Rabbi from Bezetha wanted to have the Bishop confront this woman."

"What is her sin?"

"I found no sin in her this afternoon."

"Well what are you expected to confront her with then?" she asked as she got up from the table.

James sat back from the table. "She is keeping company with a Roman soldier."

Bat-Ami raised an eyebrow. "Oh…"

"You see, even you have jumped ahead to suspect something."

She placed two cups of tea and honey on the table between them and sat back down across James. "What is it you think I have jumped to?"

"A single woman in a relationship with a Roman soldier, the assumption is probably that they are committing adultery," James explained.

"That was exactly my thought."

"You see," he accused.

"I do see," she responded, "but I fear you do not."

It was James' turn to look confused. He signaled her for more explanation.

"I jumped to the conclusion that she was being accused of sexual impropriety. I did not assume that she was guilty."

He cleared his throat. "I am sorry. I suppose that you could accuse me of jumping ahead of you."

"You suppose that I could accuse you of jumping ahead of me because…?" She left the question hanging for him to finish.

"Because," he observed, "I am guilty."

She smiled. "You apologize well."

James smiled back at her. "Practice."

"So what happened when you spoke with the woman?"

"At first she just screamed at me." He waved his arms in a wide gesture. "'Who do you think you are?' she asked me. The Rabbi and two Elders objected to the tone she used to address the brother of the Messiah. I had to keep them from making that the focus of the afternoon."

Bat-Ami nodded understandingly.

"But I could not get her question and their response out of my mind as I walked home. I did not even notice that it had rained on my shawl."

Bat-Ami frowned.

Seeing the concern on his wife's face, James tried to ease her mind. "I'm fine, really. It just feels like the pressure on me to act right has gotten worse. Either that or I am getting older and less tolerant of it."

"Act right? I don't understand."

"It wears me out, Bat, when I am asked to use the power of my position as the brother of the Messiah, or even as the Bishop of Jerusalem, to accomplish something for which my other gifts are better suited. It feels as if I am expected to be the brother of the Messiah, which just means manipulating people into submission. It sometimes feels like I am not allowed to be me." James exhaled loudly. "It is not that I would ever let the expectations of others have rule over my own prayerful wisdom. Once I have discerned the good that I ought to do, I would never let this feeling keep me from doing it."

Bat-Ami smiled warmly.

"I do not mind the thought that what I decided to do might make someone angry or disappointed. What weighs upon me is the accusation that the brother of the Messiah should be different."

"I have never heard you speak of this before James," Bat-Ami noted. "How long has this being going on?"

James shrugged. "From the beginning, I suppose."

Bat-Ami cleared her throat and asked, "Do you mean that this has been weighing upon you your whole life?"

"Not my whole life, Bat." He looked deeper into his wife's eyes. "It probably began when I first realized that Jesus was the One." He swallowed hard and looked away from his wife. "You remember that time, don't you, Bat? The time after He died but before He was taken into the cloud?"

"I remember," she said softly. "It was a very frightening and confusing time for all of us."

"Yes it was." James nodded his agreement without glancing up. "But for me it was something else." Then after pausing he looked back at his wife. "I betrayed Him, Bat. I should have known who He was, but I did not."

Bat-Ami stood again and stepped towards him with her arms extended, but James held his hand up and stopped her. After he took several deep breaths, he stood and, holding off his tears, said, "He forgave me, Bat." They stared at one another for a moment and he added, "On that day when He came to me, before He was gone...He forgave me." Having finally gotten it all out he stepped into Bat-Ami's arms and let her hold him.

They stood silently until James' breathing returned to normal. As he let go with his arms she tenderly kissed him on the cheek. Once again he held on to her and once again they stood silently.

"James?" Bat-Ami whispered, "Why have you never spoken of this to me before?"

James held his embrace but leaned back so he could look at her. "I am sorry that I haven't told you, but it has been thirty years and I could barely get it out just now."

Placing her hands on either side of his face she slowly said, "But He forgave you."

James could feel the warmth build at the top of his chest. "I know… He forgave me…but I…" He tried to look down but could feel her hands resisting. "I don't think I forgave myself."

"This does not sound like my husband," she said, leaning closer to his face. "You would never have allowed anyone else to suffer under a forgiven condemnation, James. How could you hold this for thirty years?"

"This is not guilt, Bat, truly it is not."

She leaned back, and James knew from the look in her eye that she was not convinced he was being honest.

"It is a tender memory. I do not blame myself for not recognizing Him. I could not have recognized Him until He ordained that I should. No, what I carry is the weight of knowing that when He could have used a brother's presence the most I was elsewhere."

"Are you certain that this is not guilt?"

"Yes, Bat, I am certain," he said quickly, without thinking.

Bat-Ami leaned closer again and reminded him, "You say that you are certain that it is not guilt, and you also said that He forgave you, but that you did not."

James was a bit startled. "You are right, I did say that, but I believe that it would be more truthful to say that I did not let it go rather than I did not forgive myself."

"This still sounds like guilt to me, James. Why would you not let it go?"

"Because—" He hesitated, watching his wife, and confessed, "I don't know. Maybe it is guilt. I do know that this is the memory that creeps into my thoughts at times. It sometimes feels as if this is the moment that defined who I am and what I am to do. Whenever I feel uncertain or frightened or discouraged it is the memory that returns to me."

Bat-Ami eyed her husband. "And is it the memory you think of when you feel the weight of expectations?"

James nodded. "It is."

Bat-Ami patted James on the cheek and returned to her chair on the other side of their table. Once she was seated, James sat down across from her.

As Bat-Ami held up a single finger she confessed, "I understand how you protect such a treasured memory, James, but I still do not understand what that has to do with how the expectations of others weigh upon you?"

"I do not understand it either, but whenever I am pressured to behave like the brother of the Messiah, I get flooded with all of it. It feels like the most precious part of me is being violated. I abhor using His memory like that."

"Like what?" Bat-Ami interrupted him.

James turned his head to face her squarely. "To subdue behavior and crush souls." He paused before continuing, "His memory should be used to bring freedom of spirit and courage. It should never bring fear or be used to coerce."

"I agree completely."

"What it really means to have been the brother of the Messiah is that I loved Him. He was my brother and I loved Him. I didn't know more than that." He sighed. "I did not need to know more than that." Then facing his wife again he added, "But, as His brother...I failed Him."

He could see Bat-Ami take a breath in preparation to object, so he held out his hand to stop her, "I should have been there when they killed Him, Bat."

A pained look crossed her face. "What would you have done if you had been there?"

"I know that I could not have stopped it from happening. It was His cup and He accepted it. But I could have shown Him my support, my love." He swallowed. "I could have taken care of my mother."

Her eyes were glassy as she confessed, "I did not know that you were burdened so with this...and for so long."

They reached across the table and gently held each others' hand.

"What can I do, James?"

"Please do not worry, Bat. Knowing that I have your support and love is a constant source of strength for me. It always has been." He smiled awkwardly. "It does not weigh upon me all of the time."

"But is it getting worse now?"

"Maybe it is getting worse."

"Maybe it is our age," she countered.

He examined her face for a sign that she was trying to be funny, but finding none he countered her age explanation with, "I really just want to help people. It is my calling to minister to people, but I get to do less and less ministering to people all of the time." He shrugged. "That is, no doubt, why I get angry."

"Angry?"

"My first reaction to the brother of the Messiah comments is often an angry one."

"You are not an angry man."

James nodded. "I generally do not act like an angry man, however, I do feel anger about this, and when I do, I also slow it down and remember that I too missed recognizing the Messiah as He was. How can I be angry at them when He was not angry with me?"

The concern had returned to Bat-Ami's face. "Do you go through all of that whenever it happens?"

James thought for a moment. "I think so." He looked again into his wife's eyes. He had learned that he could find compassion and acceptance in her eyes. "Forgive me if I do not tell you often enough how much it means to me that you accept me as I am." He traced a finger across the back of her hand. "I don't believe that I could keep my sanity otherwise." He watched her smile.

"I am just sorry that you feel so much pressure."

"Thank you. I don't feel this way all of the time, but for some reason today it seems worse. Sometimes my position feels more like a curse than a blessing."

"Why don't you tell that Bezetha Rabbi to...to…"

James cut off his wife's protective reaction before she said something that she would regret. "It is not his fault, my love. He is just expressing the general attitude that he was taught."

"Simply repeating what he was taught is no excuse for ignorance. Especially for a Rabbi."

"Especially for a Rabbi, Bat? I'd think that you above all others would recognize the human limitations of men who hold the title Rabbi."

She clinched her teeth. "It just makes me mad."

"Me too. And I had to stop myself from blaming him this afternoon. But he is a good man, and he is passionate and willing to act on his convictions. He may do some wrong things, but he will do them boldly and he will suffer for it. If he has it in him, he will learn as well. As for me, his expectations were really a small irritation to be persevered and normally I could have done so quickly."

"And today was different because of your weariness?"

"It had nothing to do with him. It is me. As you said, I am just getting older. It is tiring to swim upstream against the current of expectations, even when they come from well-meaning men of good faith."

"What is the name of this well-meaning man of good faith?"

"His name is Symeon. He is a young and passionate Rabbi."

"If this Symeon is so noble, then why is he so far outside of Jerusalem?"

James was a bit startled by her question. "Surely you do not presume that being closer to the heart of Jerusalem is the same as being more noble. Unfortunately, positions of leadership and prestige often go to those who can speak about their actions more eloquently than they can speak with their actions."

Bat-Ami nodded her acknowledgment.

"My father used to say, 'Don't listen to a man who speaks about what he does, watch and see what he does. For it is far easier for a man to speak the right action than to actually do what is right. The irony of religious men is that the right action is often done by those who are scorned by they who are most vocal about what should be done."

"I don't remember your father saying that."

"Oh yes, I heard him say that many times."

"And yet you feel pressure from those who are, how did your father put it, 'most vocal about what should be done.'"

"I know that it should not, but it does wear on me sometimes."

"I know that you would never let that pressure pollute you, James, but I wish it would not discourage you either."

"Did you say 'pollute'? What an interesting choice of phrases. You have a gift with words."

A loud knock at the front door startled both of them. Bat-Ami watched her husband wince as he stood and made his way to the door. She could not help but observe that he had lately been aging quickly.

A second wave of knocking startled her again. It was not unusual for her James to receive visitors at all hours of the day and night, but this knock at the door had an unusual urgency to it. She stopped in the middle of the room and folded her arms as she watched James open the door. She could hear a muffled voice she did not recognize. After a moment James turned towards her and gave her a look that meant "please be patient" before stepping into the street and closing the door behind him. Over James' shoulder, she could see the white linen tunic of an Essene.

✝

Bat-Ami was almost finished cleaning up after their evening when James returned. She continued to put the clean dishes away as she waited for him to recount his conversation in the street. As she finished with the last of the dishes, she decided that she had waited long enough.

"Well?" she said, turning to face him.

"It was Karsten. He is from the Essene community in Qumran. I am sure that I have spoken of him before. Do you remember two years ago, when the Jerusalem believers were struggling so much with feeding the brethren?"

"Yes."

"It was Karsten who organized a collection of food from their settlement in Qumran."

"I remember," she said impatiently. "And what urgent business does he have with you tonight?"

"He has brought information that Ananus is going to convene a tribunal."

Only the High Priest could convene a tribunal, which was a court of judgment. Under Roman rule there were severe limitations on the power of a tribunal; therefore they were limited for what were clearly religious issues. The High Priest had the power to appoint whomever he wished to a tribunal. As long as what a tribunal court sat in judgment over did not conflict with Roman interests, it was left alone.

"A tribunal?"

"Yes, Bat."

"Why would news about a tribunal create such worry that your Essene friend would make a point of calling on you in the night?"

"If Karsten's information is correct, then it appears that there is some secrecy about what Ananus is doing. If he were openly convening a tribunal, it might be an opportunity for open discussion.

Karsten believes that Ananus is working in secret, it could mean trouble."

"Does that alarm you?"

"It is not just that, Bat. Ananus has only been High Priest for a little better than a month, and so far he has done nothing to establish himself. He was a weak appointment, and it bothered him that he did not receive more support from outside of the Sadducees. We have all wondered when and how he would begin asserting his political position. It is a natural part of political life in Jerusalem. Ananus has to do something to establish himself in the position."

"So Karsten is concerned for nothing."

"We will know soon enough."

Bat-Ami took her husband's hand and led him through their home and outside where they could sit together under a star-filled sky and talk. "James," she said, still holding his hand, "did you say that Karsten came here from Qumran to tell you this? How far a walk is that anyway?"

"Qumran is at the north end of Lake Asphaltitis. I suppose that's about twenty-five miles west of Jerusalem. On foot it is a very long day's travel. But he did not come to Jerusalem to bring this news to me alone. He is headed to Essene hospitality house on the east end of the city. He was merely stopping here along the way."

Bat-Ami looked upward. "Do you trust him, James?"

"I do. He has taken his final vows in the Essene Rule and has been fully initiated into their Brotherhood. That is not unlike the vow I made when we married, Bat."

Bat-Ami smiled. "The Essenes do not think too highly of women, do they?"

James was taken aback by her question, and he looked at her for a moment before bursting into laughter. James' laugh was always contagious to her and soon Bat-Ami was laughing as heartily as her husband.

"No," he said as soon as he could speak, "they have that reputation, I think, because the Essenes who live at their Temples or Schools are restricted from marriage."

"Are there women Essenes, then?"

"Absolutely, Bat, and you know one very well."

"Who, James?"

"My mother."

"Mary! But I never saw your mother wear the white robes."

"She never went through the full initiation, but she did go through the first two stages. Do you remember when she caught you and Jude reading?"

Bat-Ami nodded.

"It was her Essene training that prompted her to give her blessing for your learning to read. Their conviction regarding the equality of all life is very strong. That is why they keep no slaves or even servants, and they eat no meat. They believe that men and women are equal."

"Why then did she never speak of it?"

"It is not their way to seek converts. An inquisitor must seek one of them out."

"You speak of the Essenes with such respect, James."

"I do. They are devout in their observance of the Torah, and they have a zeal for truth and justice. Karsten would have walked that far and further if he had information about an injustice, and he would have done so without regard for whomever the injustice threatened. He would rather die horribly than speak untruthfully."

"You trust his information then."

"I do not trust the news any more than he trusts it. He is simply duty bound to pass on what he knows and how he knows it. I believe he is truthfully reporting what he is told, but I have no reason to have confidence in who told him or his reasons for revealing what he knew to the Essenes."

"The information was revealed to the Essenes. That sounds suspicious to me; doesn't it sound suspicious to you?"

James nodded. "Apparently Ananus sent an emissary to Medeba to appoint someone there to tribunal. And since the hospitality of the Essenes is widely known and widely taken advantage of, the emissary probably decided to stop at Qumran and partake of it himself. The emissary was well fed and enjoyed his own supply of wine, which apparently loosened his tongue throughout the evening. The information that Karsten brought may have been nothing more than a braggart's attempt to steal for himself the illusion of importance."

Bat-Ami turned on the bench to face her husband. "Are you concerned about a tribunal being formed, James?"

"No. For all I know I could be asked to be on it."

"Do you really believe that?"

"No I don't," James confessed. "But Ananus has got to exercise his authority as High Priest pretty soon, or he might as well have not been appointed. He has to make a show of power, and he'd be smart to appoint everyone he had friction with in the past, because that would really show his power. It makes good political sense for him to send his message when Jerusalem is full for the Passover next week."

"You are sure that you are not worried?"

"I am. There will surely be much discussion at the Temple in the next few days, but in the end it will be nothing more than a show of strength and a message."

"A message to whom?"

"If I were going to send a message that I thought was important, I would send it to all twelve tribes."

CHAPTER FOUR

Regard it all as joy, my brothers,
Whenever you face various kinds of trials.
James 1:2

J ames' synagogue was on the western end of the Lower City, a five minute walk from his home, just south of the Essene Gate at the northwest corner of Jerusalem. The Lower City was not just called "Lower" because it sat below the Upper City. The inhabitants of Lower City were generally considered to be of lower status. The Sadducees lived along the Eastern Hill in the Upper City. The Upper City inhabitants referred to the Lower City inhabitants as "common." The commoners referred to the Sadducees on the Eastern Hill as "the few and the wealthy."

The Way had several synagogues throughout Jerusalem and many more around the outskirts of the city. All but one synagogue met in a house and, like the Bezetha synagogue, which met in Rabbi Symeon's house, had worship communities of between twenty and thirty believers. James' synagogue was the odd one; it was the only synagogue with its own building. It was also the only synagogue with sixty members, which meant that the size of its membership made it impossible to use this building for worship. Worship for this synagogue took place on the Temple grounds, where the synagogue was granted space on the second floor of the two-story portico along the western wall.

The synagogue building was a simple stone structure. Double wooden doors opened from the street into a single-story alcove that led directly into the meeting room where twenty men could attend worship. Above the entry alcove was enough room for fifteen women to worship. Beyond the main room were two smaller rooms; a library that contained Torah scrolls, and a study that James used as a study and for meeting with the people who sought him out for counsel.

The scholarly Pharisees had begun the synagogue movement so that Jews who were too far from the Temple could still worship, study the Torah and the prophets, and pray together regularly. Sacrificial rituals continued at the Temple in Jerusalem performed by the priestly descendents of Levi. Recently the Pharisees had built several synagogues around Jerusalem. Jerusalem synagogues were thought by the Sadducees to be unnecessary because the Temple was in Jerusalem; therefore, as long as the Jews in Israel brought their sacrifices to the Temple, their religious obligations were taken care of by the priestly elite, the Sadducees. The Pharisees built synagogues in Jerusalem in spite of the Sadduceean objections because the Pharisees believed in the priesthood of all of Israel. In synagogues, ordinary Jews could mature in their own study and purity.

James' synagogue was originally built by the Pharisees and its initial membership consisted of twenty-five to thirty Jewish tradesmen and merchants who lived nearby. It was the only synagogue whose entire membership acknowledged Jesus as the Messiah. The result of that mass conversion was that the building housed the only synagogue of The Way that had its own space outside of a home.

In its last days before becoming part of The Way, the synagogue was home to a young Pharisee named Adrian. His family had moved from Narbata to Jerusalem when Adrian was young enough to be carried for much of the two-day journey. His father, Zachary, found work as a stone mason at Herod Antipas' palace, and settled his family in the area around the synagogue where the other stone masons lived.

Adrian began his study of the Torah with the resident rabbi, Micah, who was a disciple of the Pharisee, Gamaliel. Micah had noticed Adrian's gift for scholarship and encouraged Zachary to allow his son to pursue a vocation other than his own. Adrian was fond of retelling the story of Gamaliel's prediction that if Jesus was not really the Messiah, He would be forgotten soon enough. Adrian had first heard Micah recount the story to his synagogue ten years after the Messiah's death and shortly after Gamaliel's death. 'It appears," Micah had preached, "that Gamaliel was more Prophet than Pharisee." Three months later the entire synagogue converted, giving its congregants and building to The Way.

That same building that came into view as James turned from the road leading to the Essene Gate. The double door entrance to the synagogue was shut, which was unusual for mid-morning. Normally when James found the doors shut it meant that he was the first one to arrive. That was clearly not the case this morning because Adrian was seated on a bench along the front wall to the right of the doors. The bench was normally placed closer to the doors, but it had been moved to a position immediately below an open window. As James neared the entrance doors, Adrian gestured for him to come to the bench instead of going inside. He also placed a finger across his lips, nodded with his head toward the open window, and silently mouthed the name "Bemus."

James would have been alarmed if it were not for the almost playful smile and animated gestures of his normally subdued elder adviser. In the nearly twenty years that they had been associated, James had never seen Adrian express any emotion beyond an occasional sigh or a half grin. Adrian was obviously curious about whatever Bemus was doing inside the synagogue, and as James considered what to ask Adrian, he heard the unmistakable high-pitched voice of Bemus, his other adviser.

"Of course, you don't want me to talk to your father," Bemus said, "And I didn't either."

There was a silent pause followed by a much younger voice asking, "You didn't either?" From the sound of the voice James guessed that Bemus' companion was a ten- or twelve-year-old boy, probably slight of build.

"Oh yes, Nechemya, your story is my story too." Bemus sounded boastful. "I have not always been the man you now see before you."

Another pause followed Bemus' statement. James strained back against the wall above the bench to hear better, but heard nothing until Bemus spoke again.

"I suppose that I was close to your age when I got caught helping myself to someone else's coin-purse in the Temple courtyard," Bemus said and then in a lower voice added, "It was James himself."

"The Bishop?" exclaimed the younger voice. "You lifted the Bishop's purse?"

"Ahh," Bemus responded, "so you know the Bishop of Jerusalem, do you?"

"He scares me," answered Nechemya.

James sat forward on the bench and, furrowing his brow, looked toward Adrian who once again looked like he was nearing laughter. The impulse to scold Adrian with a scowl crossed James' mind, but when he heard Bemus say, "The Bishop is scary alright...he surely is," he was startled into peering in through the window. Bemus and Nechemya were sitting next to each other not more than ten feet inside the window. Their backs were to the window, so they were not aware of their audience.

"But he is a just man, and I owe all that I am to the turn of events that began that day when the Bishop scared me."

As James settled back down against the wall, he gave a quick glance toward Adrian whose smile was no longer a smirk. It occurred to James that Adrian was making sure that James had heard Bemus' last comment before he turned away.

"And it was not the Bishop's coin-purse that I helped myself to, it was the purse of one of the Sadducee priests."

"You took the purse of a priest?" Nechemya asked in a higher voice.

"I did, Nechemya, I did," Bemus confessed with a snicker. "I was a bold one. The priest never suspected anything either until James held me by the neck and handed it back to him."

"What did the priest do?"

"He looked shocked at first," Bemus explained. "James held me up by the back of my robe so that I just stood there on my tip toes while he told the priest to check his purse. He looked embarrassed as he opened his purse to see if anything was missing. Then he looked at me like he was going to break my neck, but James asked him if anything was missing from his purse. When he told James that there was nothing missing, James swung me around and walked me out of the courtyard."

"The priest...let you...leave?"

"He did not want to let me leave. He shouted at James to bring me back, but James yelled, 'I will take care of this from here,' He did not even look back. I remember thinking, *Who is this man who has me by the neck and is so bold to defy one of the Sadducees?*"

Another silence caused both Adrian and James to strain their bodies toward the open window to hear what Nechemya might be saying.

"Yes, Nechemya, it was amazing to escape Sadduceean justice," Bemus agreed. "When James continued to walk away, the priest threatened to call the Temple guards, but James just waved his hand and kept walking. And we kept walking that way, James holding me up and me on my tiptoes, all the way back to this very room."

James smiled to himself as he remembered the event Bemus described. James' recollection did not include holding the young Bemus up to the point that Bemus had to walk on his toes, but that he held the robe tight enough to keep Bemus' from swinging his arms and darting off.

"When we got back here James asked me a few questions about my father. In fact, the questions that I asked you when we first got here were the same questions that the Bishop asked me back then. And after finding out what kind of man my father was, he took me home."

"What did your father do to you?"

There was another pause before Bemus answered Nechemya's question. James knew exactly why Bemus hesitated to respond.

"My father hugged me," Bemus said in a voice that would have sounded calm to nearly anyone but James. "I am sure that my father was angry at me, but at that moment he was relieved that I was not in the hands of the Temple guards."

"I know," blurted Nechemya. "I have never dared work inside the courtyard."

"You are undoubtedly a wiser man than I, Nechemya," Bemus said while James and Adrian smiled at each other. "After he hugged me, though, my father sent me to bed while he and the Bishop spoke. James invited us to attend his synagogue, this synagogue, and that is what we did. I think my father was waiting for someone to introduce him to The Way, and James' visit to our home was how it happened."

"Your father did not punish you?"

"Nothing beyond attending this synagogue, which did seem like a punishment to me for a year or so, but eventually I realized what a blessing it was. My father, Itamar, made his living as an artisan. He made signet ring souvenirs to sell to the pilgrims who came to Jerusalem for the three Temple festivals."

"Passover, and Weeks, and...Booths," Nechemya observed.

Without looking down James ran his thumb across the signet ring he wore on his right hand and he thought about how little the economy of Jerusalem had changed over the last thirty years. The festivals were the business of Jerusalem, and the normal population of a hundred thousand people could reach two hundred thousand during the festival times. Those who lived in Jerusalem made their livelihoods from service to the Temple or from service to the pilgrims who came to the Temple. Pilgrims had to be fed, housed, and cared for. They had to buy sacrifices to bring to the Temple and to convert whatever currency they brought for the Temple tax into the half-shekel coin that the Temple could receive. Often the pilgrims wanted souvenirs to take back to friends and neighbors. If pilgrims wanted to leave Jerusalem with a piece of jewelry, they could find no better souvenir than a signet ring made by Bemus' father.

"My father carried his rings into the Temple courtyard. It was not allowed, but the other vendors did it, too," Bemus explained. "That is what one had to do to survive. He never took his wares into the Temple itself, and he never cheated on the quality of the silver or gold. He priced his rings fairly, not doubling it, as others did, when pilgrims still had money, but the other ring makers had sold all their rings. Like many who made their livings near the Temple, he was not devout. He respected those who were devout, which did not include the Sadducees as far as he could tell, but he had no interest in it for himself. His interest was limited to his craft and his service to those who sought it."

Another silence interrupted the conversation. It occurred to James that Nechemya must have looked confused or lost because Bemus stopped the flow of his story to ask, "Did I say something confusing, Nechemya?"

"I don't know what...de-vote means," the young man confessed sheepishly.

"I'm sorry, Nechemya. It means religious or serious about observing the Torah," Bemus clarified. "And it's pronounced de-vow-t."

"I thought that you said your father was religious?"

"I said that he was waiting for someone to introduce him to The Way. That is because of something that happened to him. Once in the

Temple courtyard during Passover, the Messiah got angry and turned over the tables of the moneychangers. 'A den of thieves,' Jesus shouted. None of them argued back or even moved as Jesus went from table to table. My father said He looked completely out of control, but in the midst of His rampage through the moneychangers and vendors, Jesus looked straight into my father's eyes. Jesus looked into his face, at the string of rings he held, and back at his face. My father said he knew Jesus was treating him differently than the other vendors. When Jesus moved to the next table, my father left the courtyard. Two years later, during another Passover, my father was in the Temple courtyard and heard Peter's testimony that the man who had looked into his heart that day was the Messiah. He became a believer that day, although he claimed that he had really known the truth two years earlier. But it was not until James brought me home for discipline that my father joined The Way. My father and I shared our faith together for a year before he passed."

James recalled how Itamar had tried to pass his trade on to Bemus but to no avail. Bemus made a good vendor, but he was in far too much of a hurry to become a skilled artisan. The father had hoped that the son would share his passions, but the son had his own. Itamar never sold signet rings in the Temple courtyard again, but Bemus did. And when Bemus was not vending in the courtyard, he was helping himself to any loose coins or jewelry that he could manage to get his hands on. He knew his way in and about the Temple in a way only a mischievous child could learn. It was quite a Temple education for the ring maker's son, and that education had served The Way and the Bishop of Jerusalem well over the years. James smiled as he realized how proud Itamar would be of his son now.

James was startled from his reminiscence when he heard Adrian clear his throat. He realized that Bemus and Nechemya were standing in front of him.

"James," Bemus said in a formal voice, "this is Nechemya." And to Nechemya he added, "This is the Bishop of Jerusalem."

James extended his hand towards the young man. "Shalom."

Nechemya nodded and without speaking tentatively grasped James' hand.

"Nechemya and I are on our way to his home," Bemus announced as he placed a hand on Nechemya's shoulder.

James and Adrian stood and watched until Bemus and his young companion disappeared out of sight. Then James turned and asked Adrian, "Why were you so amused by that conversation? I thought that it was very touching."

Adrian grinned again. "You must have missed the story of how he caught Nechemya."

James shrugged. "I assumed that Bemus caught him stealing someone's coin-purse."

Still grinning Adrian said, "Bemus did not catch him."

"Who did catch him then?"

"I don't know who caught him."

Confused James asked, "How then did Bemus become involved?"

Adrian answered slowly, "It was Bemus' purse."

And suddenly James' grin matched Adrian's.

"How do you know that you can trust Karsten, James?" Adrian asked, after James had retold the details of his conversation from the previous evening. They were seated facing each other inside the large room of the synagogue.

"I have known him for a long time, and I have never known him to be deceitful in the slightest way."

"But you know how the Essenes feel about the Sadducees."

James nodded. He knew that the Essenes had left Jerusalem and established their center of worship at Qumran because they believed that the Temple had become defiled and was no longer the holy place of God, which meant that the special position of the Sadducees was outdated.

Adrian continued, "Even if he thinks he is speaking truthfully, his eyes may be blinded by his conviction that Ananus is corrupt."

James grinned.

"What do you find so amusing, James?" Adrian asked.

"Adrian, my friend," James said as he placed a hand on the younger man's shoulder, "the Essenes from Qumran may detest the Sadducees. They may even detest Ananus the most. But do you think that Karsten is any more suspicious of Ananus than you are?"

"That is different, James. I have seen him up close, and I have seen how he administered his duty as a Chief Priest before he became High Priest. My suspicion is personal and not just because he is a Sadducee."

Removing his hand, James asked, "Does that mean that you do or do not think that we should be concerned about Ananus forming a Sanhedrin tribunal?"

"I do not trust anything that that . . ."

"Please Adrian, Ananus is the High Priest. Aside from whatever he may or may not be as a man, he is still High Priest."

Adrian lowered his hand, "Forgive me, father."

"We both need forgiveness; for I have thought everything that you have said out loud."

"I have another confession, James," admitted Adrian.

"Oh?" James said inquiringly.

"I, too, heard something yesterday. And what I heard may have interfered with my ability to give due consideration to Karsten's warning about a tribunal."

"What did you hear?" asked James.

"The Romans have another Procurator on the way to Jerusalem."

"We knew Nero would replace Porcius Festus," James observed. "Do you have a reason to be concerned about who they are sending?"

"I have not heard anything other than a replacement for Festus is coming. My concern is not about the Romans, but about the Zealots. I fear what they might do with another Roman overseer on the way."

"Is your concern based upon discernment, or have you heard more than you are telling me?" asked James.

"No, James. I have told you all that I have heard. Bemus and I have noticed that neither Agrippa nor Ananus have done anything of note since Porcius Festus died. It only seems reasonable that Agrippa would be cautious now, but the High Priest has done nothing to establish himself with the people yet."

"Maybe the new High Priest is going to establish himself with the people through a tribunal," offered James.

"Maybe, James, but he would never do anything that might rile the people and embarrass Agrippa with a new Procurator on the way from Rome."

"But the Zealots would want to embarrass the King, would they not, Adrian?"

Adrian nodded. "That is at least how Bemus and I see it."

"You have thought this through well, Adrian. Although I have not thought much about the Zealots myself, I see the wisdom of your concerns. How long is it now that you and Bemus have been giving me political advice?" James asked.

Adrian blushed slightly. "You hardly need advice from anyone James, but to answer your question, you appointed me to the Jerusalem Council eleven years ago."

"And Bemus?"

"Four years ago, I think." Adrian sighed. "It seems like longer."

James smiled at the editorial comment. Adrian and Bemus were his two closest advisors, but the two men could not be more different.

Adrian was a tall, thin scholarly man of forty with angular features and a cautious disposition. Bemus was shorter and rounder than Adrian, and he was just as energetic as Adrian was deliberate. The two advisors were intellectual equals: Adrian's scholarly analysis matched Bemus' intuitive worldly experience. James knew that Adrian shared James' fondness for his younger colleague, but Bemus could wear each of them to the point of exhaustion.

"What advice do you and Bemus have for me?"

"We have not yet thought that far ahead, but that is why I am not as concerned about whether Ananus is forming a tribunal. I think that we should consider what targets the Zealots might attack and how the Romans would react if the Zealots are successful. If the Zealots assassinate Agrippa, then Nero will send another garrison to Jerusalem."

"I don't mean to argue with you, but if I were a Zealot, I would not risk Roman rule by eliminating Agrippa."

"Agrippa is Roman rule." A voice boomed from the double doorway that startled both James and Adrian. It was Bemus.

"I've just come from the Temple." He threw his shawl over a bench and approached the two men. "The new Roman Procurator is named Anthony. Word is that he is a retired military man. Stern and deliberate were the two words I heard repeatedly about our new Roman friend." Looking at James and pointing at Adrian with his thumb he added, "He sounds a bit like our old friend here, doesn't he, James?"

"Take a breath, will you Bemus?" sighed Adrian as he took a seat on a nearby bench.

"Who has time for breathing?" chuckled Bemus. "Has Adrian been telling you about our discussions concerning the Zealots?"

"Yes he has," answered James.

"Did he also tell you that the Essenes think that Ananus is going to call together a Sanhedrin tribunal?"

"No, actually I told Adrian myself."

"Were you at Temple this morning, James? I didn't see you in the sanctuary. Did you pray somewhere else?"

"An old friend of mine from Qumran came to my house last night and shared his news."

"Karsten?" Bemus asked.

"Do you know him?"

"No."

"How do you know that I spoke to Karsten last night?" James inquired.

"How does Bemus know anything?" Adrian interjected. "He heard something on the street, and then he asked someone he knows a question, and then he added two and three together and came up with the answer of nine." Then to Bemus he extended his palm. "Did I reveal all your secrets?"

"Not all of them, but it is most kind of you to ask." Turning to face James again Bemus asked, "Do you think it is possible?"

James glanced at Adrian and then back at Bemus, "Do I think what is possible, Bemus? A tribunal being formed or an assassination attempt against Agrippa?"

"An assassination attempt on Agrippa? Is that what Adrian told you? The Zealots would not choose a target of that magnitude unless they were ready for a massive retaliation." Bemus sat at the other end of the bench where Adrian sat. "Believe me, the Zealots know that they are not ready for that. But they are up to something, I am sure of it. But what about Ananus, James, what is he up to?"

"I don't know. Do you agree with Adrian that it is about time for the High Priest to assert his authority?"

Bemus looked at Adrian. "We agree about that James, but Adrian is alarmed because he does not trust Ananus."

"You are not alarmed then?" asked James.

"If I were Ananus, I would do something to ingratiate myself to the people. The new Roman Procurator will want to find out who the people trust, and if Ananus has any political savvy, he will want to give the appearance that the people love him." Bemus leaned back and added, "Our new High Priest may not have a conscience, but he has no shortage of political savvy."

"The Bishop does not care for disrespect towards the High Priest," Adrian informed Bemus.

Bemus nodded towards Adrian. "It is my tongue, Rabbi. You may take it from me whenever it offends you."

"Bemus!" James said sharply, "That is enough. The High Priest was established with the Patriarchs, and whether we like the man or not, it will be he who enters the Holy of Holies on behalf of all of Israel."

The firmness of James' voice and the expression on his face took both Bemus and Adrian by surprise. The Bishop could be tolerant and patient, but there were also lines that could not be crossed.

"I am sorry, James. You are right of course."

James moved a chair from the front of the synagogue and sat down across from his two advisors. "I am going to spend the afternoon in Bezetha again today."

Adrian leaned forward. "But James, there are things that we need to discuss." He looked for support from Bemus, but Bemus would be keeping a tight rein on his tongue for a while longer. "We have to prepare ourselves for whatever trial is coming."

In an attempt to restore Bemus, James reached out and placed his hand on his advisor's knee. When Bemus looked at him, James said, "I need you. I need you both." He sat back. "The Lord our God has given you both fine gifts of discernment, and I trust you both to do that which you have been called and equipped to do."

"And you, James?" asked Adrian.

"I will do what I have been called and equipped to do, as well."

"Bezetha?" asked Bemus.

"Yes."

"And the trials to come?" asked Adrian.

"The trials to come will come when they come."

"Rabbi, may I make a suggestion?" Bemus asked in a tentative voice.

"Certainly. What is it, Rabbi?"

"It is the timing of the trial. Anthony will not arrive in Jerusalem until well after Passover. It is likely unimportant to him. But if some trial is nearing, Passover is the most opportune time for it, no matter how you look at it. Jerusalem will be full. If Ananus wanted to win the people, then the Passover festival is the time to do it."

Adrian moved forward to the edge of his bench. "And if the Zealots wanted to rile the people up, the Passover is the time for that as well."

"Passover is only a few days away, James."

"I will not let concern about either Ananus or the Zealots worry me enough to take me away from my responsibility."

"Please James," pleaded Adrian, "your attitude towards your duty is beyond reproach but your attitude towards trials is…"

"Is what, Adrian?"

Adrian did not answer.

James looked at Bemus. He did not answer either.

James stood and placed his chair back where he had gotten it. He was aware that his advisors were watching him, and as he got to the door he turned and said, "I regard it all as joy, my brothers, when we face trials."

CHAPTER FIVE

...because you know that the testing of your faith
produces perseverance.
James 1:3

"Bishop, is that you?"

James turned and found Rabbi Symeon approaching him from the eastern courtyard of the Temple. James was standing just inside the Sheep Gate. In the hope of crossing paths with Karsten, James had taken the Sheep Gate entrance into Bezetha. The Sheep Gate led into the southern end of Bezetha and was the much longer route, but had the advantage of passing through the Temple. James had hoped that Karsten would be at Temple, but he was not.

James extended his hand toward Symeon. "Greetings, Rabbi. Are you coming from or going to the Temple?"

"As a matter of fact I have just come from your synagogue. I spent the morning at Temple, and then I went to your synagogue."

"My synagogue? Were you looking for me, Symeon?"

"Yes."

"Did you not remember that I was coming to Bezetha this afternoon?"

Symeon looked embarrassed.

"What is it, Rabbi Symeon?" James asked as he stepped closer to Symeon.

"I thought that your plans might have changed since yesterday."

"Might I venture a guess? Did you speak to Bemus at Temple this morning?" asked James.

"Yes I did, Rabbi. Bemus and I spent some time together this morning. He seems to know a great deal about Temple..." Symeon struggled to find the right word.

James finished Symeon's thought. "Bemus does know a great deal about the rumors and gossip that get spread in the Temple courtyard."

Symeon seemed to breathe easier. "Thank you, James. I was not sure how to speak honestly without sounding cruel or critical."

"I appreciate your effort, Rabbi."

A serious expression crept back across Symeon's face. "Bemus does seem concerned about some of the things that he has heard. If it is not too bold of me to ask, Bishop, are you in any danger?"

James inhaled deeply. "So he has you worried now too. I hope he does not see fit to visit my wife. That is all she will need, and then I will never hear the end of it." James looked deeper into Symeon's eyes and knew the young Rabbi was truly concerned. Placing his hand on Symeon's shoulder he added, "I am unaware of anything to be concerned about. It is Bemus' duty to think ahead in a way that would lead us to worry. But you and I are shepherds, and we have other duties. Come, let us go tend to our calling and leave those worries to others."

"But James," Symeon said without moving forwards, "he has a reasonable concern about the new Roman Procurator's arrival."

James glanced to his right and could see Antonia Fortress where the Roman Garrison was housed. The Romans knew not to meddle directly in the life of the Temple. The Syrians had made that mistake and started the Maccabean Revolution. But it made the Romans nervous to leave the Temple completely beyond their control, so they erected their fortress adjacent to and overlooking the eastern courtyard. James could see two Roman soldiers standing along the wall. Their presence was not so much threatening as it was a constant reminder of the condition of life in Israel.

"Come Symeon, let us walk and talk. I am very interested in whatever my adviser has shared with you. And I hope that I can relieve you of the undue strain with which Bemus has burdened you."

James and Symeon walked through the Sheep Gate and into Bezetha. Their conversation was sporadic until they passed the Sheep Pool, because the volume of people who recognized and greeted James made it impossible to sustain a line of thought. When they finally cleared the congestion, James initiated a resumption of their earlier conversation. "Now tell me, Symeon, what is it that Bemus told you? What is it that merits concern?"

Symeon shrugged. "He told me that Ananus hates you."

James stopped abruptly. "He told you that Ananus hates me? That is how Bemus said it, hate?"

"Yes, Bishop, that was the word that he used. Is it true?"

"Hate is a very strong word, Symeon. Did he say why he thought that the High Priest disliked me so intensely?"

"He said that Ananus was a Temple treasurer before he was made High Priest and that there were rumors that he had made loans to the Romans from the Temple treasury."

"That is forbidden, Symeon."

"I know, James," Symeon hesitated, "But is it true?"

"I am aware of the rumor, but I do not know if it is true or not. The rumor was that it was a Herodian official rather than a Roman. But that matters little except that it should remind us not to be involved with such idle and unhealthy conversations."

"Bemus also said that the rumor was never confirmed, but that they suddenly stopped because someone talked to the Sagan and that put an end to whatever was going on that fostered the rumors."

Isaac was the Sagan, the Captain of the Chief Priests. The Chief Priests oversaw the administration of duties performed at the Temple by the ordinary priests who were assigned to the Temple, and the Sagan oversaw the Chief Priests. The Sagan had the additional duty of replacing the High Priest on those occasions when the High Priest was unable to perform his obligations. The Sagan was often appointed to the position of High Priest, but in the present case, Herod Agrippa II made Ananus High Priest instead of Isaac.

"Bemus said that?" asked James without looking at Symeon.

"He said that no one knew who talked to the Sagan, but that Ananus blamed you."

James tipped his head to the side. "Bemus seems to have thought of everything. What do you think?"

Symeon cleared his throat. "I think that if Ananus does blame you, then you might be in more danger than you think."

"Symeon, even if Ananus holds me responsible for reporting him to the Sagan, do you really think that he would risk his office by using it to seek revenge against me?"

Symeon shrugged.

"Ananus owes his office to Agrippa," James continued. "Surely you do not think that he would be foolish enough to do anything that might create unrest in Jerusalem and embarrass Agrippa before the new Roman procurator gets here, do you?"

Symeon continued to walk along side of James, and without looking at the Bishop he admitted, "I know nothing of these things. The truth is, it makes my head dizzy to even think about all of this politics. I prefer to think about my synagogue and what the Lord my God wishes me to do there. I am not foolish enough to believe that I have a place beyond my call. I just do not want anything to happen to you, Bishop."

James was taken aback by the young Rabbi's words. Symeon's protective concern for James was touching, but his humility and clarity was impressive. The memory of the interactions with the young Rabbi on the previous day intruded into James' thinking. Perhaps he had been too reactive himself when Symeon had tried to protect the office of Bishop. Moving quickly from that thought to the memory of confronting Bemus for disrespecting the office of High Priest, James realized that he had better keep a closer rein on his tongue lest he crush the spirits of everyone who sought to protect him.

"Can we find a place to sit, Symeon?" asked James.

Symeon pointed to a bench near a sycamore tree and they both sat down.

"Symeon, do you remember any of the stories Peter told at synagogue before he left Jerusalem?"

"I remember many stories that Peter told before he left Jerusalem. He was a great storyteller. And he loved the Lord, did he not?"

"He did, and he was a great storyteller. It is a testimony to him that he has been so honest about his time with Christ. An honesty that has not always made him look so noble."

"May that be an example for all," replied Symeon.

"Yes. Peter's honesty and openness is truly inspirational. And it is one of those less-than-flattering stories about Peter that I want to recall for you now, if you will bear with me."

"Of course." Symeon took a seat next to where James had seated himself.

"The story that I am thinking of is when Jesus was first telling the Apostles about His death."

"And Peter said something like, 'I'll never let it happen.'"

"So you remember the story then?"

"Oh, yes."

"Do you remember what Peter told us that Jesus said to him?"

Symeon frowned. "I think it was something like, 'get away from me.'"

"He said, 'Get behind me, Satan.'"

"Satan?"

"Satan indeed." James readjusted himself on the bench and leaned forward. "Symeon, I believe that I have come to understand, at least a little, why the Lord spoke so harshly to Peter that day."

"So, why?" Symeon said with a tone of alarm that matched his expression.

"Jesus knew what His Father willed for Him. He knew and He accepted it. But I don't think that it was just obedience."

"You don't?"

"No, I don't. Obedience would have been enough for Him, but I think it was more than that. I think that Jesus knew who He was and to be anything different would have been awful to Him. Not being who He was called to be, not being who He was created to be, would have been like death to Him. Do you understand?"

Symeon furrowed his brow. "Are you saying that my concern for you is like Peter telling the Messiah to refuse the crucifixion?"

"No Symeon," James rushed to say, then paused and amended it. "Wait. I am sorry Symeon, but that is what I am saying. Peter's affection for Jesus and his desire to protect Him motivated his response, and I am accusing you, and my advisers, of having that same motive towards protecting me. It is not that your concern is wrong, but it is important that I not let the concern for what Ananus might do lead me to disobey or disregard my call. Your concern about being drawn into Jerusalem politics versus your calling as a shepherd in Bezetha is no different is it?"

"It seems different to me. The temptation to be more involved with politics is vanity on my part. We are asking you to consider a threat which may endanger you," Symeon pointed out.

"I see the difference, and you are right of course, except that no real threat has been established. You have my word, Symeon, that if a real threat presents itself, I will soberly face it. It is the Royal Law of the Torah to love our neighbors as ourselves. I promise you that I will

61

assert as much energy protecting myself as I would for my neighbor. Is that satisfactory?

Symeon nodded.

"Are you content with my protection then?"

"I am."

Standing up James added, "Shall we continue our walk?"

Symeon stood and the two of them began again for Symeon's house. "What will you do if Bemus is right about a threat to you?"

"I will do what I told Bemus and Adrian that I would do should the occasion arise."

Symeon waited.

"I told them to consider it a trial and trials should be confronted with joy. If a trial confronts us, Brother Symeon, I suggest that we meet it with joy."

"Why joy, Rabbi?"

"We must meet trials with joy because the testing of our faith teaches us perseverance."

CHAPTER SIX

You must let perseverance do its complete work;
so that you may be complete and whole,
lacking in nothing.
James 1:4

J ames and Symeon stopped talking as two Roman soldiers walked casually by, heading in the direction of Antonia Fortress. The soldier walking nearest to them looked past Symeon and nodded at James, who smiled and nodded back. Both men walked silently on until the Romans were beyond hearing distance.

Symeon was the first to speak, and he continued the conversation where it had left off, "Perseverance is a worthy virtue, James, but it is hardly that virtue which you lack."

"You are most kind, Symeon, but perseverance is the virtue of this particular season in my life. Thank you for the kind words nonetheless."

"I understand, but I do not believe that I could persevere under the conditions in which you work," Symeon confessed as he loudly exhaled.

"What conditions are you referring to, Symeon?"

"All of the politics. Why can't we get along with one another better? Do we not all try to teach our children to get along with one another?"

"Ah, I see. I have gotten so used to Jerusalem politics that I forget how polluted they are. I like the way you expressed it. We do expect our children to get along with each other better."

"Did you grow up in Jerusalem, Symeon?"

"Yes, very near to where my home is now. My parents lived in Bezetha before the wall around it was built. My father worked for the owner of an olive vineyard south of the city. He operated the press."

James studied him. "What is your father's name?"

"Eli was his name, and my mother's name is Yaffa."

"His name...was...Eli," clarified James.

"My father died ten years ago. He has found his place in the next kingdom and we rejoice with him, although we miss him dearly."

"And your mother?"

"She still lives in their home. You passed by it yesterday as you left my home," answered Symeon.

James nodded. "I did not know your father, Symeon, but I think that I remember him. I believe that he was one of the early converts. Is that correct?"

"It is. Mother heard the Messiah teaching on the hillside the day He performed the miracle of the fishes and loaves."

James grinned. "She ate some of that food, then."

Symeon grinned too. "No, she did not. She saw the miracle, but she was too afraid to eat of it herself. She still regrets that her fear got the better of her that day."

Symeon continued, "She told my father everything that she had heard. When Jesus came to Jerusalem, they went to hear Him teach at Temple. I believe that they would have followed Him when He left Jerusalem." He lowered his head and his voice. "But He never left Jerusalem again."

"Did your parents ever speak of those early days?"

"My father spoke of the early days when there were so many converts in Jerusalem that there was a problem feeding them all."

"Yes I remember now. Your father was involved with organizing the distribution of food, wasn't he?"

Symeon looked pleased that James remembered. "He was."

"Your father was a tireless worker. You are right to feel proud of him."

Symeon smiled.

"Did Eli tell you about the persecution that followed those days?"

Symeon crunched his eyebrows. "Persecution?"

"A year after that Passover when the Messiah was crucified, Peter spoke in the Temple courtyard and there were three thousand converts. The Way was overrun with new brethren, and they all wanted to stay in Jerusalem. Most of the converts were circumcised, but many were not. The uncircumcised converts presented a problem for us. Do the Gentile believers have to be circumcised? Do they have to follow our laws about what is clean and what is not, or about honoring the Sabbath in the manner that we were taught by our ancestors?"

"The real issue," continued James "was the relationship that the uncircumcised converts had with the Temple. Those days were harsh, but The Way held an accepted position with the other Jerusalem sects because we held on to the traditions and laws of the Temple."

Symeon stopped walking and turned his body to more directly face James, "Do you mind if I ask you another question about our interaction yesterday?"

"Please do."

Symeon paused and stared at his hands for a moment before starting to speak. "I did notice yesterday that you were less than pleased with us when we—" he stopped speaking and, looking up at James, he corrected himself—"I mean, you were less than pleased when I rebuked Mary for raising her voice at you."

James folded his hands on his lap and waited for Symeon to continue.

65

"At first I thought that you objected to our, I mean *my* interference." Symeon tilted his head to the right. "I assumed that you simply preferred to be left alone, to respond to her in your own way."

James nodded.

"But—" Symeon rubbed his hands together—"when you told the story about the Lord rebuking Peter, I realized that your reaction was more than that."

This fanned the flame of James' curiosity. He had not realized how much Symeon had noticed the day before. "Go on, Rabbi."

"As I understand the exchange, the Lord rebuked Peter because Peter was attempting to alter the Lord's destiny. Is that right, James?"

"Well said. Was that the question that you wished to ask me?"

"No, Rabbi, the question I want to ask is much more personal."

Extending his right hand, James beckoned Symeon to proceed.

"I cannot understand why you told that story then, Rabbi, except for it being somehow similar to what happened when I rebuked Mary yesterday. But I have not discerned how my doing that interfered with Mary's destiny. Or was it your destiny?" Symeon shook his head slowly, "If it is not too personal, would you please help me understand my offense?"

"You have taken in much more than I had realized, Rabbi Symeon. It is true, there was more in my flinch than I have shared, and it is personal. That is why I bear you no offense, because there is no reason for you to know that it would affect me as it did."

"What was it that affected you?" Symeon spread his hands apart. "I do not even know that."

"It was the reference to me as the brother of the Messiah."

Confusion crossed Symeon's face. "But...you are the brother of the Messiah."

"I am."

"I do not understand."

"It is not being referred to as the brother of the Messiah. That is who I am, and I consider it a blessing." James rubbed his lip with the tip of his tongue. "No, my reaction was at how my relationship to the Lord was invoked."

Symeon straightened up and leaned back slightly. "It is what you called it yourself."

"That is true, I did. But I did not mean to offend you."

"I know you did not. You saw something that merited a correction and you corrected it immediately."

Symeon relaxed his shoulders a bit.

"I understand that when you searched for a way to express your rebuke the use of my kinship to the Messiah was immediate and powerful."

"I merely thought it would make her think more soberly about her uncomely display."

"And to that end, I am sure that it did...but do you not see that instead of slowing her tongue out of maturity or discernment, she may slow it out of fear of whom she speaks to?"

"If she acts more righteously—"

"If her actions are more righteous," interrupted James, "because she is afraid of the brother of the Messiah, then I am nothing more than a weapon. When people invoke my title as Bishop of Jerusalem to coerce subjugation it feels as if they are using me like a club. And when the same thing is done with my kinship to the Messiah, it feels even worse."

"If the Bishop title could be used as a club, then the brother of the Messiah relationship is a spear."

James looked deeper into Symeon's eyes. The young Rabbi had surprised him again. "Yes, it can be used as a spear. And my relationship to my brother is far too personal to be used as a spear. But the intrusion into my family is only part of the reaction you noticed." Raising a finger James asked, "May I explain more?"

67

Symeon nodded.

"I have been Bishop of Jerusalem for over twenty years. I have no regrets about my office. It is worthy work, and I have been blessed with the opportunity to serve the Lord's Kingdom in this way." James sighed. "But it is not what I would have chosen for myself."

Symeon did not hide his surprise. "It isn't?"

Shaking his head James confessed, "All I ever wanted to do was help people."

"What do you helps multitudes of people."

"I know it is important work." He smiled. "But the work I really enjoy is ministering to people individually, personally."

"That is why you came to Bezetha instead of sending another, is it not?"

"It is." Then in a softer tone he added, "The demands that the growth of The Way has placed upon me has conspired with the complexities of Jerusalem politics to keep the opportunities for personal ministry further from me."

Pausing, James gave Symeon the opportunity to speak, but seeing no movement in that direction, James continued, "Ministering to people, like Mary, during their trial times is also important work. And if I can say without boasting, the Lord our God has blessed me with gifts for that ministry as much as for the work as Bishop."

"Tell me, James, this ministry that you are speaking of, is it something that I should know more about?" Symeon asked, with a serious look.

"Why do you ask, Symeon?"

Symeon turned and began walking again "I have been the Rabbi of my own synagogue for over a year now. For many years I have ministered to people with the Torah. People would ask me to advise them about what the Torah says, or ask me to offer prayers or blessings for them. But for the last year I have found that on several occasions my ministry to people lacked something. It is always during, what did you call them, trial times?"

"I think I know what you are speaking about. As Rabbis we advice, we instruct, we exhort, and we intercede. These are all activities that we can do to or for the people we minister to. But there are other times when what people need is something other than what we do."

"What?" Symeon asked.

The memory that came to James' mind made him smile. "I once heard it referred to as *chanuck*."

"*Chanuck?* Is that not what midwives do for babies? It is what parents to for their children." Then Symeon remembered. "It is Solomon's wisdom too."

"Yes."

"Train up a child in the way he should go and when he is old he will not depart from it."

"That piece of Solomon's wisdom is precisely where the term came from."

Again Symeon's forehead wrinkled. "I know that midwives train by using a sweet mixture of dates and honey to coat the gums of some babies to get them to suckle."

"That is precisely what it means."

"And I know that the term is sometimes used about parents who nurture the—" Symeon seemed to struggle to find the right word —"the soul of their children. Is that how you mean training, James? To nurture growth by using what the Creator has already placed within the child even if it is immature and incomplete?"

"You have defined it well, Symeon. Training up a brother or sister into maturity is a calling that makes use of the naturally occurring tendencies that The Lord our God placed within the souls of His people. Things like hungers, pains, hopes, fears, responsibilities, desires, needs, and all sorts of other tendencies can be an important part of how we mature. It is these things that are acquired and

69

strengthened as we face one trail after another. These things can be polluted (he used the term he received from Bat-Ami the night before) as we grow but trials can reveal the pollutions that should be overcome."

Symeon nodded, then tipped his head towards his left shoulder. "You believe that Mary is in some kind of trial, don't you, James?"

James nodded. "Yes, I do."

"And you believe that the trial is why she has begun keeping company with the Roman soldier."

"Now that relationship is something that I do not know about. What I do believe about Mary is that something in my question was threatening or hurtful to her and I am curious about whatever it is."

"Could it simply be an unconfessed sin?"

"I suppose that she might have reacted the way that she did if she were hiding a sin. But the speed of her reaction to my question leads me to suspect that a wound of some kind is more likely to blame."

"What kind of wound?"

"I do not know, but whatever it is will continue to get in the way of her growth and maturity until it begins to heal. And that, my brother, is why I want to pursue my ministry to her."

"Thank you, Bishop. This is a valuable lesson for me." Symeon folded his arms. "When did you first borrow Solomon's term to describe your calling?"

James hesitated and slowly turned to face the horizon to his left. Symeon could not have known what distant memories his question would call forth in James. "It was not my term," James finally said. "It was Saul's term."

"Saul?" Symeon asked in a startled voice. "The Apostle to the Gentiles...that Saul?"

James was surprised by how startled Symeon appeared to be at the mention of Saul's name.

"The Saul who Herod Agrippa sent to Rome?"

"Symeon," James interrupted, "why do you find it so hard to believe that it was Saul who named my calling?"

"I apologize, your grace. I did not mean to sound like I was questioning the truth of what you said." Symeon held his palms out. "I do believe you, I just...could not..." He looked down at his palms, as if searching for a word.

"Visualize it?" James suggested.

"Yes." Symeon put his hands on his legs. "That is it. I could not find a way to put the picture of Saul speaking to you that way in my mind."

James looked away and nodded. "I am afraid that our brother Saul did not enjoy the support of the Jerusalem brethren towards the end of his ministry." James inhaled deeply and sighed. "And I am afraid that it is more our shame than his loss."

Symeon did not ask a question, but neither did he appear to understand to what James had made reference.

"You mentioned the event in which Agrippa and Festus sent Saul to Rome," James noted. "Do you know how it came to pass that Saul found himself in Agrippa's custody?"

Symeon shook his head.

"As you already mentioned, Saul was called to minister to the Gentiles," James began. "And no more faithful servant ever lived."

"Not a more faithful servant than you, Bishop," Symeon objected.

"That is kind of you to say, Brother Symeon," James answered, "but hardly true. I have been as faithful as I know how to be, but Saul was called upon to give his life for the sake of the Gospel. And he proved worthy of that calling. I have enjoyed the support of the Twelve Tribes in Jerusalem and the comfort of a calling within the comfort of my homeland. Saul spent his calling in foreign lands, often in poverty, and sometimes in chains. And all the while his faithfulness to the Gospel was salted with the suspicion that he was unfaithful to the Torah."

"I have never heard harsh words spoken of Saul," Symeon offered.

"But that was a time in Jerusalem before yours, Symeon," James countered. "And even in the absence of the harshness, the reputation you have been exposed to has not had the affection and respect from the Jerusalem brethren that Saul deserves."

Symeon nodded.

"I think that it grieved him that his devoutness was questioned here. That is why he returned to Jerusalem from Ephesus, to answer the charges that he had taught the Jews scattered among the Gentiles to turn away from Moses."

"I did not know this."

"The charges were false, Symeon, but they were serious. One rumor in Jerusalem at that time was that Saul had said that he considered his circumcision to mean nothing more than *skubala* (refuse), but when he was here he clarified what he had written in an epistle from a Philippians jail that his circumcision was *skubula* in comparison to the Gospel." James looked at Symeon. 'It was a misunderstanding like that which fueled the rumors and suspicions."

"But he was exonerated from those charges when he returned, was he not?" Symeon asked.

"He was. When he returned to Jerusalem he immediately came to the Jerusalem Council and reported to the elders. He submitted to the Council's authority and followed our instructions as we directed him to go to the Temple and demonstrate his observance of the law by going through purification rites and paying the Temple taxes."

"Saul submitted to the authority of the Jerusalem Council?"

"He did."

"Saul submitted to your authority as Bishop of Jerusalem?" Symeon asked pushing further.

James hesitated. The question, as asked, made him uncomfortable. But Symeon appeared to be asking about Saul's submission more than James' authority, so James answered simply, "He did. It was Saul's submission to those instructions that placed him in the Temple where a riotous crowd seized him and drug him from the Courtyard."

"Because of the rumors?" Symeon asked.

"Yes, and they may have killed him, too, if the Romans had not arrested and taken him away."

"And is that arrest how he found himself in Agrippa's court?"

"It is."

Symeon leaned his head toward James. "Is that when Saul gave you the name *chanuck*?"

"It was after his arrest. I visited him several times a week while he was held in the barracks of Antonio Fortress," James clarified. "At first we spoke mostly about the goodness of the Lord and of how different our callings were." James smiled in embarrassment. "We each had several things to confess about our lives prior to knowing the Truth. Eventually we began to speak of more personal things. I am sure that if our positions had been switched, he would have ministered to me, but as it were, it was I who had the opportunity to minister to him."

"What was it like ministering to Saul?"

James shrugged his head forward. "Saul was used to being mistreated. He expected beatings and imprisonments wherever he went. As I mentioned before, he was willing to spend his life for the sake of the Gospel." James extended his hand towards Symeon. "Truly, he expected to die." Turning his palm up he added, "Being willing to spend your life for the Gospel does not mean having no fear about it."

"Saul was afraid?"

"Of course he was afraid, and hurt and a bit confused by the treatment he received from his brothers here."

"What did you say to him?"

"I let him express what he felt and I avoided telling him things that he already knew. He wept at times, pounded his fist on his bed at

73

times, and once he screamed in anguish. Each time he expressed himself in these ways, I simply stayed nearby."

"That is all you did?"

"Does it sound so simple?" James asked as he laughed. "I suppose that it is simple, even easy, to be present when another is expressing himself in the manner in which their body and soul were created. The more difficult task is to hold the tongue when those expressions violate your own comfort or sensitivities."

"How did Saul benefit from that?"

"That is an interesting question, Symeon. On my last visit with him, Saul asked me the same thing. He said, 'I feel more peace within myself after we talk, but I do not know why.'" James turned his head to more squarely face Symeon, "I do not know if I fully understand it even now, but I remember what I told Saul that day."

"What did you tell him?" asked Symeon as he turned to match James' posture.

"I told him The Lord our God had made our bodies and our souls to function in certain ways and that those natural ways of functioning can become polluted by the world. This I believe happens to us all, but pollution does not take away God's intention within us; it merely covers over it."

"So when one acts in accordance to God's intention, it feels natural even if it is unfamiliar because of pollution," Symeon excitedly projected.

"Yes, Symeon, that is it." James smiled.

Symeon, with a pleased expression, sat upright. "I presume that is when Saul referred to your ministry as training."

"*Our* ministry, Symeon," corrected James.

"Our?" Symeon's confusion reappeared.

"Brother Symeon," James began, "I suspected that you might have a bit of this gift when I realized how much you had observed and noticed about me earlier. But the speed and clarity with which you have grasped the idea of training convinces me that it must be a gift you have at least a portion of. Maybe that is why the Lord has placed Mary in both of our lives."

Symeon's shoulders dropped and he looked away.

"What is it, brother?" asked James.

"Before we go, can I confess something?"

"Certainly Brother Symeon. What is it?"

"You were right, James. About wanting you to confront her. I do not know if she is in sin in this relationship, but I do believe that it is a dangerous one that could easily become sin. Confronting her was for her best. She is ruining her reputation with the brethren."

Her reputation or your? Thought James. "You may be right about what is best, Symeon, but it is her life. How can you be sure that God is speaking to her through you? How can you be sure that what you think is best for her really is best for her?"

"Is it not our job, our responsibility, to know what is best?"

"It is our responsibility, at all times, to seek to know the best and to encourage others to do so too."

"That is exactly what I want for Mary."

"Is it?" James asked.

"Of course. How could I wish for anything else?"

"If Mary is sinning against her Lord or her neighbor, is it better that she be stopped by those who know what is right, or is it better for her to stop herself because she comes to recognize what is right?"

"As long as she stops sinning, then it does not matter." Symeon hesitated. "Does it?"

"I suppose that the answer to that question depends a great deal upon whom you ask."

"I would like to know what you think."

"I think equipping her to take responsibility for her life as she lives it for God is best. And I answer that way because I believe that equipping her is what my call to ministry is about. Mary is a resourceful person. I am sure that she is capable enough to take responsibility for her life. She will need help at times, but any help that overrides her responsibility is not help at all."

"I suppose that means you will not tell her to stop visiting with the Roman," declared Symeon.

"I will not tell her that unless I discover, for myself, that they are sinning. What if it isn't true?"

"What if?" Symeon stood up and flung his arms upwards. "What if they are sinning and she lies to you? What about that?"

"If she is lying, then her sin will get worse, her guilt will increase, and she runs the risk of more and more complicated consequences."

"That is your answer: Her guilt will increase?" Symeon's voice squeaked.

"It is," James said calmly. "Do you disapprove?"

"I do. According to that, people can just keep making the same mistakes over and over until they learn the lesson."

"This is precisely what I think."

Symeon turned and faced James with his hands on his hips and sarcastically asked, "How is failing over and over again until you learn your lesson supposed to help anyone grow in their faith?"

James looked directly into Symeon's eyes. "You must let perseverance do its complete work; so that you may be complete and whole, lacking in nothing."

CHAPTER SEVEN

If anyone lacks wisdom he should ask God
who gives generously to all without finding fault.
James 1: 5

J ames and Isaura arrived at Mary's open door early in the
afternoon. Mary's home was a single room with a cooking area
under an open-walled shelter beyond the back door. A bed rested
along one wall and was covered with piles of clothes. Mary sat at a
table in the middle of the room mending a shirt. She was humming to
herself, but stopped suddenly when she noticed James in the doorway.

"Greetings, Mary," James called from outside. "Do you remember
me?"

Mary stared at the open door for a moment, then lept to her feet and
rushed towards the door saying, "Please come in."

"Have we come at a bad time? We did not actually set a time to get
together again, but I did not want to put it off after upsetting you so
yesterday."

Mary looked at him as if she did not understand, "It is I, sir, who
should be apologizing to you—" she lowered her head—"for yelling at
you the way I did. I should never have acted so badly."

"Nonsense. You were clearly bothered by my question. I did not
take your reaction personally. It is I, not you, who needs to make
amends. So, what do you say? Will you give me another chance?"

Mary looked at James and then at Isaura and then back at James.
"You are most kind, sir, and you are welcome in my home, but I don't
know what you mean by another chance. Another chance for what?"

James smiled. "That is a good question. It appears that neither you nor I knew why we were called together yesterday."

Mary looked again at Isaura, who had still said nothing since arriving. Mary searched Isaura's face as if to find answers to questions that she was afraid to ask James directly.

Noticing their interchange, James said, "I trust that you remember Symeon's wife, Isaura. She was good enough to join me while I visit with you."

"Hello again," Mary said meekly to Isaura. "Can I offer you something to drink?"

"Hello, Mary. Thank you for the offer, but I am fine right now," Isaura said to Mary. Then, after glancing at James, she added, "Please do not fuss about me. You two go ahead and talk. I will be fine to sit here out of the way. If you don't mind, I did bring some mending to do."

Mary swept her arm around the room. "I don't mind at all. If you finish your mending, I am sure I can accommodate you."

Isaura looked at the piles of mending around the room. "I would love to help. I just brought my mending so I would not be in the way."

Mary looked embarrassed. "No, no, I couldn't do that. Each pile has different requirements, and I am on schedule, so thank you, but I think that it would be better for you to take care of what you brought."

Isaura looked at James for direction.

"That was a very nice offer Isaura, thank you." James nodded towards Isaura's basket and watched her take her mending out before turning to Mary and smiling. "Now Mary, you told me a little about yourself yesterday, are there any questions that you have about me?"

James noticed that Mary looked down and he assumed that she was unsure of why he had come. "You are aware, I think, that I am a rabbi. And I think I was introduced to you as the Bishop of Jerusalem."

"Why would the Bishop of Jerusalem come to see me?"

"I thought I was being asked to offer you some counsel?"

Mary looked down at her lap where she was still holding the shirt that she had been mending when James and Isaura arrived.

"Please, Mary, do not let my visit interfere with your mending. I insist that you continue working while we talk."

Mary took up her mending. "Thank you. I can listen while I work," she assured James. "What do you mean by counsel?" Her hands nimbly worked a needle through the fabric before her. She looked comfortable at her labor.

"Rabbis teach their people what the Torah says and encourage the people to obey the Torah. When a rabbi is with his congregation, he preaches to the people, instructing them in what the Torah says, but sometimes a priest or a rabbi guides an individual in applying what the Torah teaches to their lives."

Mary had finished knotting her repair to the shirt that she had been mending and bit through the thread. She picked up a robe and was searching through it for the tear, but James' last comment caught her attention. Placing the robe back into her lap, she looked squarely at James and asked, "Apply…what the Torah teaches?"

"Yes, Mary." James waited and watched her as her focus seemed to move from James' face to somewhere over his right shoulder.

When she seemed to return she asked, "Would you explain more about…?"

"Applying the Torah?" James finished her question. "Yes I can do better. Let me try it this way; people go through trials all of the time. Some trials are easy for them to solve and others are more difficult. Sometimes people can face trials that they need help to endure. Or they wonder how the Torah can help answer a question they can not answer. I often help people at those times."

Mary sat up a little straighter, which encouraged James that he had finally found the right words. He continued, "Usually the person who is asking for help comes to see me. But in this situation, your rabbi, Symeon, asked me to help you."

Mary's shoulders slumped again. "Help me? Are you here to help me?"

"Now it is my turn to be embarrassed, Mary. I gather from your question that you did not know that I came to Bezetha yesterday to help you. And that is why I have returned today."

"To help me?" Mary repeated.

"Yes, helping you was my desire," James said, "and I believe that helping you is the reason that Symeon asked me to come as well."

"But…" Mary glanced at Isaura, who was keeping her hands busy, but without the skill or effectiveness with which Mary mended. Then, looking at James out of the corner of her eye, she asked, "I did not ask for help. I do not mean to be rude, but I do not need help."

James leaned as far back in his chair as he possibly could and placed his hands on his knees. "I apologize to you, Mary, if our assumption that you needed help has offended you."

"Rabbi," Mary interrupted him, "I have taken no offense. The truth is that this is a lonely time in my life. I have only been in Jerusalem for a short time. I do not know many people here and there is much that I do not understand about living here, I think my status as a single woman makes everyone suspicious."

"And our attempt to help, before you asked for help, has not made this lonely time any easier for you, has it, Mary?"

Mary did not answer.

"I would like to offer you my help. And the help I would like to offer first is that I can and want to pray for you. Would you accept my offer?"

Mary hesitated, and then softly said, "I don't want to be a burden to you."

"Praying for you would hardly be a burden. Besides, tending to the sheep of the Lord's flock is the only part of being the Bishop of Jerusalem that I really enjoy."

In a stronger voice, Mary asked, "Will you allow me to pray for you as well?"

James fought off the urge to smile. He felt a fatherly pride in her desire to pray for him, but he was unsure of how she would interpret it. "I would be honored if you would pray for me, Mary. Thank you."

Isaura dropped her mending and scrambled to pick it up. James reached to help her, but Mary was closer and retrieved the shawl from the floor.

Isaura accepted the bundle of cloth from Mary without looking at her. "Thank you."

"You do nice work," Mary said as she handed over the garment.

Again Isaura said, "Thank you" without looking at Mary.

When Mary settled back into her chair, James continued, "Mary, if at any time you become aware of anything that I could do to make me more spiritually complete, no matter how trivial or how important it is, then I invite you to speak of it to me boldly. Will you do that?"

Mary studied his face again, "I will. And I hope you will do the same for me."

"Well then, shall we begin?" James asked. "Maybe I could answer some of your questions about living in Jerusalem."

Mary stared back at James and sheepishly said, "I do not know what to ask. When I was a small girl my family would travel to Jerusalem for Passover every year, but I only came once. I was no more than seven or eight." She paused as she pulled a thread taut through a knot and bit it off close to the knot. "I remembered the Temple being much larger and the people much grander."

James had heard similar observations before. For most people who first view heavenly things through the faith eyes of a child, there is an expectation of how adults will be that inevitably brings disappointment and sometimes disillusionment. Maturity in faith must pass through this trial sooner or later. Maybe this was the season for Mary.

"The Temple was the dwelling place of God our Father throughout much of the history of our people," James said, "It is still a place where we worship Him and honor the traditions of the Patriarchs. But it is also a place where the people of God have responsibilities, and that means it is vulnerable to our frailties and flaws. Greed, ambition, jealousy, even ignorance can all be found where men gather, even in the Temple Courtyard. In Jerusalem there are seven sects and each one has different ideas about the Temple. You know who the chief priests are, do you not?"

Mary nodded yes while she picked up another shirt to mend.

"The chief priests are Sadducees. They are descended from the tribe of Levi and they were given the responsibility over the sacrifices in the Tabernacle while we wandered in the desert. They still have that responsibility at the Temple now that we are settled in the land God promised Abraham."

"The chief priests are holy men."

Isaura's cough drew glances from James and Mary, but she did not look up from the mending in her lap.

"The Sadducees are men. Some are good and devout men, other are...less so."

Without looking up from her mending Mary asked, "Did you not say that there are seven other sections?"

"Sects," James clarified. "There are seven sects in all. Six beyond the Sadducees."

"If some Sadducees are unfit, then why can't one of the other sects replace them?"

"It is not so simple to replace the ones God has anointed," James answered. "Each of the other sects undoubtedly thinks about the place of the Sadducees differently. Take the Essenes, for instance." He paused. "Do you know of the Essenes?"

"Oh yes," Mary answered, glancing up from her lap. "There was an Essene hospitality house in Tiberias."

James nodded in acknowledgment of Mary's observation. "Originally the Essenes were part of the priesthood, but they separated from the Sadducees years ago when they were persecuted by what they refer to as a 'wicked priest.' That is why they call Qumran home. The Essenes believe that the Sadducees and the Temple are defiled." He pointed at Mary. "They agree with your sentiment that the Sadducees should be replaced, but they choose to wait instead of directly disposing the Sadducees themselves."

"Are the Pharisees a sect?" Mary asked.

"As a matter of face there are two sects of Pharisees: Hillel and Shemmi." James wiped his mouth, "The Pharisees have great respect for the office of priest, but they believe that Israel should be a nation of priests. The Sadducees believe that the Holy Place of the Lord our God is within the building of the Temple, but the Pharisees believe that the Holy Place of God is within the chosen people, the nation. The Pharisees built synagogues all over Israel so that the people of God could worship and study the Torah away from the Temple."

Mary's eyes narrowed. "The Pharisees were trying to replace the Sadducees."

"I had not thought of it quite like that, but I believe that you are right, they were." James grinned. "And that reminds me about a third sect connected to the Pharisees, the Zealots. They were originally Pharisees."

"Really?" gasped Isaura.

Isaura's exclamation brought Mary's eyes up from her lap again.

"Yes really. They, like the other Pharisees, believe that the Sanctuary of God is in the nation, not just the Temple. That is why they consider Roman presence anywhere in Israel to be an outrage."

Mary leaned forward and, as if to be careful, she whispered, "I heard that they are assassins."

"I have heard that, too," whispered James in return. "Is there anything else that you would like to know about the sects?"

Mary counted the fingers on her left hand. "I thought you said there were seven sects. We have only talked about five."

"That's correct, forgive me. The other two sects are the Way and the Herodians. I take it that you already know about The Way so let me just explain the position of the Herodians. They are Jews, at least by birth, and they hold governing positions by appointment from the Romans. They would never attempt to replace the Sadducees because the people would never accept that from them and if the people revolted then the Herodians would no longer be of any use to the Romans," James finished by taking another deep breath.

"Thank you, Rabbi," Mary offered. "I will certainly think differently the next time I am at the Temple."

James continued, "You told me about your family yesterday. Is there anything that you'd like to know about mine?"

"Are you," she hesitated, "married?"

Out of the corner of his eye James saw Isaura flinch at the question. If Mary noticed Isaura's reaction, she did not show it.

"I am married. My wife's name is Bat-Ami."

"Do you have children?" Mary asked.

"We do. We have two sons, Leander and Nicholas."

"Are they both—" she looked at Isaura and then back at James —"are they living?"

Isaura kept working but peered at Mary over her mending.

"They are. Leander lives here in Jerusalem and Nicholas lives in Lydda. Do you know where Lydda is?"

Mary shook her head no.

"Lydda is about twenty-five miles northeast of Jerusalem." James started to point, but he got confused so he added, "It is just about ten miles this side of Joppa."

Mary nodded in recognition.

"Is there anything else you would like to ask me?" James asked.

Mary shrugged sheepishly.

"I have a question for you if you don't mind."

"I don't mind," Mary said.

"I still don't know what it was that I said to you yesterday that upset you so much." James put both of his hands up, as if surrendering. "Not that I am asking you to tell me anything that is too tender or too personal to talk about. But I didn't want to let it just pass by us either. Whatever it was that upset you yesterday when I asked how you came to Jerusalem must be important to you. When you are ready to talk about it with me, then it will be important to me as well."

Mary looked away. "It isn't important."

"I don't think that you would have reacted so strongly to something unimportant. At least most people wouldn't."

"Well, it doesn't really matter, anyway," Mary said hurriedly.

"What leads you to say that it doesn't matter? Is it too painful still? Or does it seem hopeless to talk about?"

"The past is the past. It can't be changed, so why talk about it?"

"True enough. As a matter of fact I make just that point to many of the people that I talk to. Sometimes people get so focused upon what happened in the past that they miss what God is doing in their lives right now." He watched her closely. "It's good to hear that you aren't thinking that way at all."

Mary kept still and maintained eye contact with James.

"There are other ways that the past can make us miss the opportunities that the Lord our God affords us today. When we have strong feelings about something that happened in the past, then sometimes those feelings can blind us."

"How does talking about it help? What happened still happened."

Raising his finger, James noted, "But it does not have to feel like it is still happening. Talking about it doesn't change the past, but sometimes it helps keep the past in the past."

Mary looked at him suspiciously.

"It is like Job," James said nonchalantly.

"Job! The man who lost his family?" Her eyes tightened. "Are you going to tell me that losing my family was a—a—test?"

"We are speaking about the same man, but I am referring to a very different part of his story."

"Go on."

James continued, "I am referring to Job's lament, which comes well after he loses everything. It is the time when he says something like; 'I have concealed my sin as men do...'"

"Are you accusing me of concealing a sin?" interrupted Mary.

"No Mary, I am not accusing you of hiding a sin. Listen to the rest of his lament, please. It will make more sense when you hear all of it."

"I'm sorry," she said, "I will not interrupt again."

James started quoting Job again. "I have concealed my sin as men do, by hiding my guilt in my heart because I so feared the crowd and so dreaded the contempt of the clans that I kept silent and would not go outside.'"

Mary's head gently rocked back and forth.

"Did you recognize that passage?" James asked.

"It is not a common passage for worship, but I have heard it before," Mary observed.

"Did it make sense to you?"

"I think so. Job knows that he has to be careful because people will talk." Mary snarled. "Gossips and busy bodies don't care who they hurt. They are like dogs." She stiffened and made a fist. "No, jackals. They are like jackals."

James knew he had once again hit a nerve. "So you see why Job was so adamant about hiding anything he thought would result in contempt?"

Mary's chin stiffened in determination. "Absolutely."

"Would you not say this is why we have a tendency to keep secrets?"

"Is that what you think, Rabbi?"

"Yes, Mary, it is what I think. I think most of us have some secret or other that we are hiding from everyone else. What do you think?"

"I guess that is true."

"So you agree with me that Job's lament speaks for all of us. You agree that we all fear rejection, scorn, and contempt?" James asked.

Mary nodded.

"And do you also agree that we keep secrets as a way to avoid those painful things?"

"I agree."

James leaned forward. "Do you know what the next verse is in Job's lament?"

Mary shook her head no.

"The next line is, 'oh, that I had someone to hear me!'"

"Oh that I had someone to hear me?" Mary repeated.

"Apparently if you hide all your secrets you won't be rejected, but no one will know you. And then you will long to be known."

"Are you saying that secrets are bad?"

"Not exactly. Keeping a secret is sometimes the wisest choice if we are keeping it from the wrong person. I know that people have a hard time controlling their tongues. And I know that the tongue can do an awful lot of damage."

Mary nodded her agreement.

"But there is a consequence to the keeping of a secret, especially if you keep it from everyone." James sat back. "It keeps us from being known."

"And what is the benefit of being known?"

James was impressed with her willingness to challenge him, but he also knew her bravery may be more related to protection than courage. "Would you say that everyone desires to be accepted by others?"

"Yes."

"And would you say that being accepted by others is so important that we might keep a secret in order to ensure our acceptance, our place with others?"

"I suppose."

"Do you see the dilemma than? We want to be accepted, but if we pretend to be someone else in order to get accepted, then we won't really feel accepted."

Mary excitedly interrupted, "Because it won't be the real person who is being accepted. It will be the false person that is accepted."

James watched Mary think. He was spiritual director to many people and this moment of recognition was one of his favorite moments.

Mary looked at him again. She appeared to be sizing him up. "You have convinced me. I agree that there are consequences to keeping secrets. But that does not mean that every secret should be told, does it?"

"No it doesn't. I don't think every secret needs to be told and the ones that should be told don't have to be told all at once," answered James.

Mary smiled. "You think that I have a secret, don't you?"

"I do, Mary, I honestly do. And I think that your secret has something to do with why you came to Jerusalem."

Mary's face was expressionless, but that in itself was revealing. Her breathing was also very shallow. James noticed and asked, "Would you prefer for me to stop?"

"You can go on. I am curious about what you are thinking."

"Okay, then I will just add that I also think that whatever happened in Tiberias involved your being hurt by people you now think of as jackals."

Mary watched James intently as she wiped her lips with the palm of her hand. "You are right. In everything that you said, you are right. The good women of Tiberias made it impossible for me to stay there.

It was contempt that they showed me, and it is contempt that they deserve."

"Do you feel contempt for them?" James asked.

"I know that I shouldn't," Mary answered crisply.

James waited.

"I know that I should forgive them." Mary looked down. "But I can't forgive them. I've tried, but in my heart I cannot do it."

"Have you prayed about it?"

"I have. I prayed that God would change my heart. But it hasn't changed." Her eyes teared up slightly. "I prayed in Tiberias for God to change those jackals, and I have prayed in Jerusalem for God to change me, but He has not answered my prayers yet."

"Did you pray for relief or for wisdom?" asked James.

"Wisdom?" Mary paused and stared at James. "Praying for wisdom never occurred to me."

"It does not occur to many of us, especially when we are in the midst of a difficult time, but that is when we need wisdom the most." James paused to allow Mary to respond, but when he realized she was remaining quiet he continued, "It is natural for us to want painful circumstances to stop. Therefore it is also natural for us to appeal to our Heavenly Father to give us relief as only He could."

"If only He would," Mary blurted out as she looked away.

James took a deep breath before continuing. "I know it can be frustrating and disheartening when the relief that we pray for does not come."

Mary slowly turned back to face James.

"God our Father does not always relieve us of trials or suffering, but He is faithful to us, which means He has a redemptive purpose in everything that He does, including what He allows."

"Am I to be thankful for my suffering?" Mary asked sarcastically.

"Not for your suffering but hopeful for your place in the Kingdom to come and hopeful for whatever purpose is being worked out while you suffer. These are the times that test our faith."

In a softer voice Mary asked, "Am I to understand that you think that when my faith is being tested I should pray for wisdom instead of relief?"

James held his hands out. "Not instead of relief, Mary, but in addition to relief. We should pray to our Father about all things on our hearts, including relief. After all, one of the ways that God may grant us relief is to give us the wisdom to discover relief that He has already provided." He lowered his left hand. "I have just come to recognize that most of us have to be reminded to pray for wisdom."

"Even you, Rabbi?"

James smiled. "It is in me that I have recognized this the most. But I am getting better at remembering to pray for wisdom for myself as I get older."

Mary nodded. "Praying for wisdom…that is what you think I should do?"

"I do, Mary. I think that if anyone recognized that he lacks wisdom then he should ask God for it."

CHAPTER EIGHT

But when he asks, he must believe and not doubt,
because he who doubts is like a wave of the sea,
blown and tossed by the wind.
That man should not think he will receive anything from the Lord;
he is a double-minded man, unstable in all he does.
James 1:6

"Isaura, you have been most quiet all day," James observed as they left Mary's house and began their walk back to the home Isaura shared with Symeon.

"Yes sir," Isaura said in a quiet voice.

"Are you normally so quiet, or have you been instructed to be quiet while you are with me?" James asked, aware that she might also be quiet out of being afraid of him. Being treated as if he were unapproachable was one of the many drawbacks of his reputation.

"I am normally quiet, but I also knew to stay out of the way while you spoke with Mary. No one told me to be quiet; I did not want to interfere."

"Well Isaura, I appreciate your willingness to let Mary and me visit. If it were not for you, then she would need to come all the way to my synagogue in the Lower City. I do not think that she could manage that, do you?"

Isaura shrugged.

James answered his own question. "She is a widow and makes what is probably a meager living mending. The half a day's time that it would take her to come to my synagogue would cut deep into her livelihood. As it is, I am sure that just visiting with me will cause her to work into the evening."

"She should be grateful for the time that you give her," said Isaura.

"I am sure that she is grateful."

Isaura looked away from James.

"Do you disagree?" asked James.

Isaura turned slowly to look at James. "I do not think that she behaves with as much respect as she should."

"I find it refreshing. She treats me honestly. She doesn't trust me much yet, but she is open and responsive to what I offer her. She will make me earn her respect." He made a fist and extended it. "I like that."

Isaura kept her eyes forward as she continued walking.

"Do you think that Mary should treat me differently because of who I am?" James asked in a lower voice.

"Yes sir."

"May I ask you a personal question, Isaura?" He slowed his pace.

She slowed her pace a bit to match his.

"Do you treat me differently because of who I am?"

Isaura stopped suddenly, a look of terror across her face.

James stopped too, "Isaura, please, I did not mean for my question to disturb you. It is just that so many people treat me as if I am not an ordinary man."

"But you are not an ordinary man."

"Because I am the Bishop?"

Isaura nodded. "And the brother of the Lord."

"Aah! The brother of Jesus."

"My lord, I am sorry."

"No, Isaura, it was not you. It's just that being Jesus' brother is not an easy thing to think about."

"My father died when I was still young, and I grew up with an older brother who was as much a father to me as a brother."

"Jesus?" Isaura asked.

"Yes. We did not know that He was the Messiah. I was at a wedding when He performed His first miracle, but even then I did not recognize Him as the Messiah."

Isaura appeared horrified by the confession.

James continued, "I loved Him, Isaura. I loved Him with all of my heart, but I did not recognize Him. He was my big brother. No better big brother ever lived. He always encouraged me, built me up. I was mischievous, but Jesus was never harsh with His discipline." James giggled to himself. "He never rescued me from the consequences of my misdeeds, either. I remember there was one time when . . ." James noticed the expression on Isaura's face and decided that so familiar a story of Jesus would be more than she could bear. "Oh well, that story doesn't matter right now. I grew up fairly normally. My father died when I was fourteen, so my mother was a widow, but she was well cared for by my brother. None of us recognized Jesus, except maybe Mother. If Mother did recognize that He was the Messiah, then she buried it in her heart."

Isaura listened intently.

"People treat me differently today. It is as if I have some power or insight based on my family, my childhood. They want me to have the Lord's insight. But I don't. I am an ordinary man, Isaura, in an extraordinary position. If I got something special out of my childhood, and I did, it was that my brother loved me and encouraged me to be myself." A tear rolled down his cheek.

Isaura looked away.

"Thank you for listening to me, Isaura."

As Isaura turned back to face him, he added, "Might I ask another favor of you?"

"Anything, lord," Isaura said, eyes widened.

"Would you treat me like an ordinary man who is trying to be faithful?"

"I will try, but I am not sure that I know what you mean exactly."

"You could answer questions honestly without regard for my position or family."

Isaura hesitated. "I will try."

James smiled and nodded. "Do you know why we were at Mary's home today?"

"No sir, I don't."

"Well the elders of your synagogue believe that she may be in a relationship that is filled with temptation. They want me to confront her and convince her to give up that relationship."

"Is that what Symeon believes?" Isaura asked.

James was surprised that Isaura needed to ask what her husband believed. "Yes it is. Has he not said so to you?"

"No sir, Symeon has never spoken to me of such things. Do you believe that she is—" Isaura stopped and tentatively added —"sinning?"

"I do not know. What do you think?"

"She seems like a hard woman, sir." Isaura shrugged. "But that does not mean she is guilty. Does it?"

"No Isaura, it doesn't. That is a very good observation."

Isaura smiled and turned her head away.

"Isaura let me ask you for another observation. What do you think the synagogues ought to do for the widows and orphans in their domain?"

"I don't know, sir."

"Do you have any thoughts about the treatment of widows?" James asked.

Isaura took a deep breath. "There was a woman who lived near my family. She was a good woman. Hers was the most contagious laugh at the well when the women would gather in the morning and share stories. She was the favorite of my sister and me."

"She sounds delightful."

"But her husband took ill and in less than a month she was a widow." Isaura looked down. "She moved soon, and it was years before we saw her again." She looked back up at James. "My sister and I thought that she was living with relatives or something, but when we saw her, she was a street beggar near the Temple."

James wanted to reach out and touch her shoulder, but he knew that gesture would be too familiar. "It is the sad story of many, I am afraid."

"My sister and I spoke of it often. How easy it is for a man to lose a wife. But for a woman it is very different. She did not deserve what happened to her. The sickness that took her husband could have taken anyone's husband."

"So you can have compassion on Mary?" asked James.

"Oh yes, indeed. But she scares me a bit, too."

"Really? What do you find scary about her?"

"I have never seen a woman speak to men the way that she does."

"She is a strong one, that is for sure. But is that not a quality that might serve her well? In her circumstances, it is not surprising that she is a big of a fighter."

"I had not thought about it that way. Speaking so boldly always seemed dangerous to me. She could get herself in serious trouble if she spoke to the wrong man that way," observed Isaura.

"That is true, she could." James paused and lifted a finger. "But maybe she learned that speaking softly caused her more trouble than speaking boldly."

"How do you mean?" Isaura asked.

"I mean that since we do not know about the trials that Mary has endured, we do not know what she has learned or what she believes she must do to survive. Mary may have been very meek at one time. And she may have been betrayed or hurt as a result of her meekness."

"It is hard to picture Mary as meek."

"But it is not hard to picture a widow, like Mary, being treated in a manner that hardened her, is it, Isaura?"

"No, it is not. But isn't meekness a virtue that we should seek, even if we are treated badly?"

James was surprised at Isaura's depth. "Yes it is, Isaura. I suspect that it is a virtue that you have developed in yourself."

Isaura's head pulled back slightly. "Not I, lord. If meekness is a virtue that I possess, then it has come to me by God's blessing and not by my own hand."

James nodded. Isaura responded as a meek person would respond. "Amen, Isaura. If you have the gift of meekness, it is because our Father in heaven has given it to you. But to your credit, you have been a good steward of the meekness you have been given."

A blank expression crossed Isaura's face.

"Anytime you felt wronged or slighted you could have hardened your heart against the meekness that the Lord our God had given you."

"But those are the moments when meekness is most important," Isaura stated boldly, but in a softer tone added, "Aren't they?"

"Well said, Isaura. And your meekness has grown in each and every one of those moments. Has it not?"

"I suppose so," Isaura admitted begrudgingly.

James stood up, "Since we have reached a point of agreement, shall we continue walking?"

Isaura stood up and they began walking again.

"Might I ask a question of you, sir?"

"That would be fine. What would you like to know?" offered James.

"Well, since you asked me why we were visiting Mary, let me ask you the same question: Why are we visiting Mary?"

James stroked his beard before he answered, "I came to Bezetha to try to offer some help to Mary. My life in Jerusalem has become more about maneuvering for political power than I feel comfortable with. I look for chances to minister to God's people." James looked forward again. "Anyway, after the first meeting with Mary, I realized that she is wounded. I believe that I can help her with that wound."

"I saw no wound, sir," Isaura observed.

James thought for a moment about Mary's reactions to his questions. She had reacted much more strongly to the question about coming to Jerusalem than the questions about her family. The feelings that she had displayed when speaking of the death of her husband and son were strong but straightforward and congruent with what he expected considering the circumstance. Her reaction to the other question was much more curious. "The wound is in her heart, I think. I am not sure yet, but somehow I feel that her wound is not from the loss of her family, but from the events that followed that accident." He frowned. "Please do not repeat what I have said. It is pure speculation. Even if it does turn out to be true, it is not something that Mary is ready to reveal to me yet."

Isaura pressed her fingers to her lips. "I can keep a secret, sir. But before we get to my home, I have another question, if you please."

"By all means. What is it?"

"You told Mary to pray for wisdom?"

"Yes."

"You told her it would be given. You guaranteed her wisdom."

"I guaranteed that she would receive wisdom if she asked for it, but it is not I who will give it to her."

"But you guarantee that she will get it."

"I guarantee that it will be given...not that she will get it."

"I don't understand. If Mary asks for wisdom—"

James interrupted. "Not just Mary. Any woman, any man."

"If a man asks for wisdom, he will be given wisdom but he might not get it. Is it that simple?"

"It is that simple. If a man asks for wisdom, his Father in Heaven will give it. But when he asks for wisdom, he must believe that God will send it. If he asks with doubt, he should expect nothing because his double-mindedness will prevent him from recognizing wisdom when it appears. That man will remain unstable in all he does."

CHAPTER NINE

The brother in humble circumstances ought to take pride
in his high position. But the one who is rich
should take pride in his low position,
because he will pass away like a wild flower.
For the sun rises with scorching heat
and withers the plant:
its blossom falls and its beauty is destroyed.
In the same way, the rich man will fade away
even while he goes about his business.
James 1:9

J ames noted to himself that this night the walk home from Bezetha did not seem nearly so long as it seemed the night before. He felt better about his work and his service. *I truly feel the most alive when my faith and my work fit together.* It was a common thought and a common theme that James spoke upon at the synagogue when he taught. But today his faith and works fit together so well that he wondered if it might have actually eased the aging pain in his knees as he walked home.

James arrived at his door still enjoying the momentum of his time with the widow, Mary. He was delighted to have accomplished some real work instead of the usual business of settling disputes between theological factions or playing politics with the seven sects or looking over his shoulder for Ananus. James reached his door, touched the *mezuzah*, and paused to recite the *shma*.

The door swung open just as he finished his prayer. Bat-Ami, who must have been listening and waiting for him to finish, considered James with an expression of concern. She stood to one side of the doorway and watched him notice that there was a man sitting inside.

After a day of listening to suspicions about secret Sanhedrin tribunals and the plotting schemes of the Zealots, seeing his friend Nathan startled James. Nathan, a devout Pharisee, had a position on Herod Agrippa II's staff as a court adviser and bureaucrat. The Pharisees had an agenda for bringing their own particular interpretation of the Torah to the entire Jewish nation, but they did not possess the Levitical bloodline of the Sadducees or the appointed position of the Herodians. The lack of an inherent position meant that the Pharisees had to be politically astute and, more importantly, they had to be useful to the ruling power...at the moment, the Herodians. The Pharisees were useful to the Herodians because they were more respected by and connected to the common people. Nathan, in particular, was useful to Agrippa because of his level head and sound judgment.

James had not been too concerned about Ananus and the possibility of a tribunal being formed, but Nathan's presence in his home alarmed him. Ananus had been appointed by Agrippa and would not risk doing anything that might get the King's disapproval. If Ananus was forming a tribunal, then Nathan would likely be on it. Nathan was not the highest ranking Pharisee in the Hillel house, but because of his position with Agrippa, he was the most politically influential Pharisee in Jerusalem. If Ananus were forming a tribunal or doing anything else that was a threat to James, then Nathan would waste no time in getting word to James.

James' friendship with Nathan had begun shortly after Paul left Jerusalem for Rome. Paul had appeared before Herod Agrippa and Festus, the Roman Procurator, to plead his case after he was arrested and imprisoned. But instead of arguing for his innocence, Paul had used the opportunity to proclaim the Gospel. Festus accused Paul of being crazy from too much studying. Agrippa chided Paul for using the trial to spread the Gospel. Festus and Agrippa were not convinced to the point of believing Paul's testimony about the Messiah, and they would have released Paul, had he not demanded a trial in Rome. Nathan had been present for all of Paul's orations, and he been one of those to whom Agrippa himself had said, "This man is doing nothing that deserves either death or prison, if he hadn't appealed to the Emperor, he could have been released." Shortly thereafter Paul was sent to Rome, never to return to Jerusalem.

It had been nearly eight years since Paul's last journey to Rome. Shortly after Paul's departure for Rome, Nathan came to James' synagogue asking the Bishop questions concerning the Way and its Messiah. Agrippa had become curious and sent Nathan to find out more about this belief that Paul had been willing to die for. It was not long before Agrippa stopped sending Nathan to find out more about the Way; Agrippa had either lost interest or had been swayed to give it up by his sister, Beatrice, with whom he had an incestuous relationship. But Nathan had continued to visit James for his own reasons, none the least of which was the mutual respect and friendship that he had developed with James.

"Ministering to the poor, James?" Nathan said as he stood up and approached James with his hands extended.

James relaxed a bit as he heard the familiar chide from Nathan. "If I could exhort like you then I would not need to spend so much of my ministry on my feet, my friend."

They embraced with a hug.

"How are you, James?"

"Busy, but good. My knees keep reminding me that I am aging."

"But no man has done better work on his knees than you." Nathan stepped back and added, "James of the Calloused Knees. It is a reputation you have earned."

"And tell me how you are, Nathan, and what brings you to visit Bat-Ami and me?" James stepped towards his wife and put an arm around her.

"I miss you, James. Bat-Ami tells me that you were tending to a widow out beyond the Fish Gate."

"She did?" He kissed Bat-Ami on the cheek and watched her excuse herself. "That's true. I was." He motioned for Nathan to return to his seat.

"Sometimes I am in awe of your passion for ministry, and other times I wonder about your use of time."

"Time?" asked James.

"The time you spend with a widow is time that you might be able to do much more good with if you spent it on those more . . ." Nathan hesitated.

"Worthy?" James offered an end to Nathan's thought.

"Influential is what I was going to say," corrected Nathan.

"Influential?"

"Don't play coy with me, James. You know exactly what I mean."

James spread his arms in mock innocence.

"I am not a heartless man, James, but I am a practical one. How much influence do you think a widow has?"

"Well, I think that she had a tremendous influence on me."

Nathan rolled his eyes. "I mean, how many people is she responsible for? How many people answer to her or rely upon her?"

"I don't know, Nathan, maybe none."

"None. But if you had spent the afternoon with a merchant who influences many or one of your own priests, then that time would be multiplied by what they do with what you did."

"It sounds to me like you equate influence with rank."

"Of course."

"There is no doubt that rank carries a certain influence over any that fall beneath that position. But that kind of influence can be limited to the behavior rather than the heart."

"The heart follows the behavior, James," Nathan said as he waved a finger.

"True, but sometimes the behavior follows the heart. Passion will lead men where law cannot and passion does not get communicated down through rank but laterally through relationship."

"So, how many relationships does the widow have?"

"I don't know, and I don't care either."

Nathan raised an eyebrow. "You don't care?"

"Not really. What I care about is her...and I suppose me, too. You see she has a need, and I seem to be able to meet it. The timing and circumstances that put us together leads me to believe that it is the Lord our God's will for me to minister to her. And that is what I care about above all else."

"That it is God's will?"

"Yes," said James.

"Shall we shift our discussion to the discernment of God's will? To evoke 'it is God's will' into this discussion is to close the discussion. How can I question God's will?"

James shrugged.

"But I can question your discernment. And so I ask you, by what basis do you discern God's will?"

James thought a moment. "Doing the good I know to do. How do you base your discernment of God's will?"

"By the law, James, the law. God has spoken to us through the law and where God was silent, we have the authority of oral tradition."

"So you consider that the discernment of God's will about ministering to widows should come from the Scriptures?"

"Or the elders."

"What about the words of Isaiah, or Jeremiah, or Ezekiel? Are those authorities enough for you?" asked James.

"Did they tell you to minister to this widow?"

"Not this widow, but each one of them condemned the religious authorities of their day by pointing to their treatment of widows and orphans."

"You are taking that very personally, James," observed Nathan.

"How else is it to be taken, Nathan?"

"It is an indictment of the entire community. The religious authority of the day was not conducting itself in such a way that the ministry to widows was occurring."

James stroked his chin. "And if the religious leaders had been doing what they were supposed to do, then the widows would have been ministered to by whom?"

"By the adherence to the law. By their families and the good will and charity of the communities where they lived. The right things happen when the Law is held in its proper place."

"And while families adhere to the law and communities are charitable, what are the religious leaders doing?" asked James.

"Running the synagogues, teaching the law, and administering the sacrifices."

"And doing that will make the people do what is right on behalf of widows?"

"It is what is required of us by law."

James shook his head. "It is not working."

"That is dangerous talk my friend."

"It was dangerous talk for the prophets. They were all killed for what they said. How is it dangerous for me? I am not condemning anyone of anything. I am just discussing the discernment of God's will with an old friend."

A much more serious look washed over Nathan's face.

"What is it, Nathan? What is on your mind?" James said, leaning forward.

Nathan answered without lifting his head. "I didn't just come here this evening to visit with you."

"No?" James said in his most innocent voice. "What is on your mind, Nathan?"

Nathan leaned closer and lowered his voice. "I do not know who else I can talk to, but I need to talk to someone that I can trust."

"What can I do to reassure your trust, my friend?" James asked.

With his voice lower still Nathan explained, "I have heard some alarming conversations at court, and I need to know that we will not be...overheard...by anyone."

James flinched with realization. "Are you speaking about Bat-Ami?" James looked toward the rear of their home and wondered what she would say if she had heard what was being said. "Nathan, are you concerned about my wife overhearing us?"

Nathan scooted out to the edge of his seat. "Please forgive me, James. I do not mean to insult you or Bat-Ami. I know that I must seem foolishly cautious, but I fear I must be with what I am about to share with you."

"No offense taken. I am sure that you have good reason to be cautious, and I can assure you that Bat-Ami is not trying to listen to us." James sat back in a more relaxed posture and added, "I can also guarantee you that she will ask me about our conversation, and that she will respect my wish that she not speak of it."

"Thank you for understanding." Nathan nodded.

"Now tell me, what can I help you with?"

"The tension in the Palace has been quite high since Porcius Festus died. Herod Agrippa's appointment came from Nero himself, but a change in the Procurator is still a time of adjustment. We have only heard rumors about who will be sent, but no word from Rome has come."

As Nathan continued his story, James wondered about Bemus' source for his information that the next Procurator would be a retired legion commander.

"Agrippa's temper has been short with everyone, but no one has received more of his ire than the new High Priest."

"Ananus?" James asked.

"Surely you are not surprised, James?" noted Nathan.

"I am surprised. I had assumed that Agrippa and Ananus were allies. Why else would he have appointed Ananus as High Priest?"

"I believe that Agrippa considered Ananus to be more controllable than the Sagan would have been. Ananus has always been more involved at the Palace than the Temple anyway, so if Agrippa needs to unleash his anger at someone that he knows will take it, Ananus is his man. I suspect Agrippa is also a bit provoked about Ananus' relationship with Beatrice."

"What is his relationship to Beatrice?"

Nathan waved his hand. "Ananus spends more time catering to her than reporting to Agrippa. Agrippa thinks of the new High Priest as Beatrice's pet and he despises him for his weakness."

"I had no idea. It makes me feel a bit more sympathetic towards Ananus," said James.

"I would not suggest letting him into your confidence just yet, James. He is a weak man who knows that his position comes from power that is not his own. Ananus will take whatever Agrippa unleashes upon him, but he is High Priest, and he is not above using his position for his own gratification."

James nodded.

"About two weeks ago, Agrippa and Beatrice asked the advisers to anticipate any difficulties that the change in the Roman Procurator would bring. We all seemed to predict the same difficulty."

"Let me guess," James said. "You all predicted that the Zealots would seize the opportunity to make trouble."

"Exactly." Nathan reached forward and gently tapped James on the shoulder. "I know that it was not a particularly difficult prediction to make, but a Zealot plot is still the most worthy concern for the Palace right now. We always expect trouble from them, but we expect something bigger right now."

"Have you some specific trouble in mind?" asked James.

"We did generate a list of targets that we thought the Zealots would be likely to attack. Their goal will be to cause as much embarrassment as possible to King Agrippa. But that list is not what concerns me, James."

"What is it then that concerns you, Nathan?"

"After we presented our list to Herod Agrippa he summoned the High Priest to meet with him."

"Agrippa wanted advice about the Zealots from Ananus?" James speculated.

"Not advice, James." Nathan's face grew more solemn. "Agrippa asked...no, he ordered the High Priest to make sure that the Zealots were under control."

James sat still.

Nathan waited a moment for his friend to digest what he had just told him before continuing, "I know how you feel. It is incredible to expect the High Priest to control the Zealots. Ananus was speechless too when Agrippa told him to get it done."

"I would think that Ananus would have objected to having his office used for such purpose," observed James. "Agrippa is not a devout Jew, but he must have some idea about the High Priest. He cannot be unaware that he is degrading the office of High Priest."

"Oh, he is serious enough. He does not understand the High Priest's position regarding the sacrifices, but he does understand position and leadership. To King Agrippa, Ananus holds the highest religious position in the land, and he wants Ananus to use it to control the people. In Herod Agrippa's world, it is the nature of political position."

"Did Ananus protest?"

"He tried, as did we all, but the King would hear nothing else. He was as adamant as I have ever seen him. I found myself wondering if Agrippa had been promised that the High Priest could deliver peace between the seven sects."

"Ananus would not have been so foolish as to promise that, would he?" speculated James.

"I do not know, James, but the whole conversation was bizarre. Nothing about it made sense to any who heard it."

James scratched at his beard. "What do you think Ananus will do?"

Nathan sighed deeply. "That is why I am here, James. I do not know what he will do next, but I know what he has already done."

"This is sounding more serious, Nathan."

"Ananus sought advice from Beatrice. They met two days ago."

"What is the nature of their relationship?" wondered James.

"I am curious about that myself. I do not know if she had some influence over Ananus' appointment to become High Priest. Or maybe Ananus hopes that her relationship with Herod Agrippa will protect him when he fails to control the Zealots."

James raised an eyebrow. "It is hard to imagine that Beatrice has some insight into the politics of the Zealot cause."

"She had an opinion, James." Nathan stared at James and waited until he had James' undivided attention. "She told him that to control the Zealots he would have to control The Way."

"What!" James exclaimed. "She can't be serious. What is she thinking?"

"She thinks that The Way is gaining support and converts more than the other sects in Jerusalem."

"What does that have to do with the Zealots?" exclaimed James.

108

"She told Ananus that the mass of converts to The Way was making the Zealots angrier."

"Beatrice knows that the Zealots are only concerned about ridding Israel of the Romans. Why would she tell Ananus something that she does not believe herself?"

"I don't know, James, but I do know that she has never been comfortable with what she calls the 'Messianic cult.' I really thought that Agrippa was moved by listening to Paul before they sent him to Rome, but I think that it was Beatrice who discouraged the King's interest."

"Why would she do such a thing?" asked James.

"James." Nathan shrugged as if to imply that the answer was obvious. "She remembers the story about the Baptist and his attack on Herod Antipas' adulterous affair with his brother's wife."

"I see," said James.

"She is always nervous, James, whenever she is in the presence of anyone who proclaims the Messiah."

"It is her own guilt that condemns her. It comes from within her own heart that condemns her. It is not The Way."

Nathan raised his hands. "I know."

"But what of Ananus? He could not have accepted her proposition."

"The High Priest said nothing."

"Ananus said nothing when Beatrice told him that The Way was responsible for the anger of the Zealots?"

"He said nothing," Nathan repeated.

James ran his right hand through his hair. "What do you think that Ananus will do?"

"Again James, I have to say that I do not know, but I heard something today that made me suspicious that Ananus is putting together a tribunal. I know a Pharisee, Nathaniel. He is a *Shammi;* you have probably seen him at Temple, but you may not have ever spoken.

He is suspicious of The Way and frets over the growth of your converts."

"I think I know whom you mean. Does he have a very young face?"

"Yes, James, that is him. He is fairly new to Temple life. Yesterday he asked some of us about what being on a tribunal would be like. He denied being asked, but I think that someone must have inquired about his disposition towards The Way."

"And what do you think his disposition would be?"

Nathan looked over his should for Bat-Ami. Not seeing her he said, "Not good, James."

"So, do you think that we are in danger?"

"I think that there is trouble coming, James. The Sadducees have the power now and they seem to be setting up a display of it. I don't think that it is more than that, but I do think that The Way is the target."

"My wife is worried about my safety. Do you think she has reason?"

"No. It wouldn't get that bad. Even if Ananus was capable of such larceny, the other sects would never allow it. They are good, learned men with great responsibility. They seek to protect the faith and tradition of God's people and they are concerned by what they see. You can understand, can't you, James?"

James sighed. "I can understand."

"Well, I'm glad. I was mostly concerned that you would be caught off guard. I'm sure that you have some concerns."

"I have no concerns about talking to the Sadducees, but what if they want me to do something?" James asked as he stroked his beard.

"Do something like what?"

To avoid answering Nathan's question James said, "I cannot believe what a bad host I am. Nathan, please forgive me. I have not asked you about your wife. How is Eliana?"

"Eliana is well, thank you for asking. She and I will be leaving Jerusalem before Passover."

"A trip for pleasure?"

"No, I will be visiting the synagogue in Jericho; Eliana will accompany me and visit her sister. She lives in Jericho."

"That will be nice for both of you. Will you be there through Passover?"

"Yes, that is the point, after all. The master of the Jericho synagogue can take Passover in Jerusalem if one of us replaces him there. It is my turn."

"If I am not mistaken, going to Jericho means that you are sacrificing your position for another of lower rank."

"James." Nathan laughed. "You are relentless."

James smiled. "And you are more interested in serving the humble than you say."

Nathan stood up and shook his finger at James. "I had better go before your famous flattery persuades me to join The Way."

"I pray that you will, Nathan, but not by flattery."

Nathan reached out and laid his palm on James' arm. "I must go."

"Good-bye, Bat-Ami," Nathan called towards the back of the house.

Bat-Ami appeared in the doorway. She was drying her hands with a towel.

"Good-bye, Nathan. Please come back anytime."

"I will." Nathan bowed. "Your hospitality is only surpassed by your graciousness."

Bat-Ami bowed her head back and smiled.

"Now James—" Nathan grinned—"keep ministering to the humble."

James just smiled. "I am not certain that it is the humble who need us the most, Nathan. It may be the powerful, whose influence will last no longer than a wildflower in the scorching sun, who needs ministering the most."

CHAPTER TEN

Blessed is the man who perseveres under trial,
because when he has stood the test,
he will receive the crown of life
that God has promised to those who love him.
James 1:12

James chuckled to himself as he watched Nathan walk away down the street. He was still grinning when he shut the door and turned to face Bat-Ami. He could tell that she had questions, and she was not to be denied.

"What?" he asked.

Bat-Ami folded her arms and said nothing.

"Nathan thinks that Ananus is going to convene a Sanhedrin tribunal," James admitted.

"How many people have said that to you now?"

"Nothing is certain, Bat."

"James, a man in Essene robes came to our door last night after walking half way across Israel just to tell you the High Priest is forming a tribunal and now Nathan tells you the same thing. Tell me the truth."

"There are rumors floating around Jerusalem, but no one knows what they mean. It's probably nothing more than political retribution."

She rolled her head away from him.

"It's going to be fine, Bat-Ami," James said in his most reassuring voice.

She turned her head back sharply and stepped closer to him. "Can you assure me of that?"

James hesitated.

"I didn't think so." She turned her body away from him.

He stepped closer and put his hands on her shoulders. "Please don't be afraid."

She wiped something from her face.

"I love you with all my heart," James said into her ear. "Do you know that?"

She nodded but did not turn.

"Is that not enough?"

"No, James, that is not enough." She turned around, "We are getting old. Is it not time to let someone else be Bishop of Jerusalem?"

"You want to go and never return. What would you have me do, Bat?"

Bat-Ami clutched his forearm with both hands. "There is not a synagogue anywhere away from Jerusalem that would not welcome you, James. We can grow old and fat. You could write."

"I could write!" said James with a start. "Write what?"

"Write about what you are passionate about, about what you speak about, and devote your ministry to."

"And what would that be, Bat-Ami?"

"In one way or another you are always encouraging the people of God to find their true selves by living out their faith in every aspect of their lives." Bat-Ami put her hands on her hips. "You know that I am right, James. I hear you from the back room, I have been in the synagogue every time you have taught, and I have saved some of your notes."

"My notes?" James questioned.

Bat-Ami walked over to a cabinet and removed a handful of papers.

"What do you have there?" James asked.

"I have pages that you worked on before you spoke in the synagogue." She handed him the one on top. "Here's something that you wrote about faith and works."

James took the page from her and looked at it.

"You see," she said in a smug voice, "that is what you are passionate about."

He looked up from the page. "I'm no writer." He held out the page, "At best, this is no more than an essay."

"It doesn't matter how long it is. What matters is that it is important to say. And you say it better than anyone."

"Spoken like a wife," said James.

"Some wives may see their husbands as the heroes they want to see." She paused and stared at him. "Do you think that I am one of those wives?"

James just smiled as if the question was rhetorical.

Bat-Ami pressed the question. "Well?"

"No, Bat-Ami, you are not one of those wives."

"Then kindly respect my opinion of your writing." Bat-Ami demanded.

He nodded. "How many of those essays do you have anyway?"

She counted through the pages. "I have eight here, and the one you have makes nine. Here is one on not showing favoritism and there is another one in here on taming the tongue."

"That's interesting." James noted.

"What?"

"That the one you remember is the one on taming the tongue."

"This is no time to be funny, James," she said sharply.

"I'm sorry. Writing is a good idea, even if nothing comes out of it. But I do not want to think about it until after Passover. Is that acceptable to you?"

"After Passover! You aren't planning on leaving Jerusalem, are you?"

"No."

Bat-Ami sat down.

James sat down across from her. "The timing to leave is all wrong. Adrian and Bemus are able elders and ready to lead the Jerusalem synagogue, but neither has the passion for ministering to persons that the Bishop of Jerusalem needs. My successor will be surrounded by administrators, it is the natural order of things, but The Way needs someone who will remember the people as well as the congregation."

"Maybe one of them could develop that attitude, James, if you gave them the chance," offered Bat-Ami.

"Maybe they could, but more likely the next Bishop will come from a smaller synagogue. In fact, I believe that I have met a young Rabbi who has the passion for ministry. In fact, he is the Rabbi who invited me to Bezetha."

"Are you grooming him to replace you?"

"I am encouraging him to grow in wisdom. He has passion. He sees a need and he charges at it like a bull. He is the elder who asked me to confront that widow I've been visiting. If he learns to slow down a bit he might be perfect."

"And then can we leave Jerusalem?" Bat-Ami pleaded.

"That is not the only reason that I feel called to be here at this time."

"What else keeps us here, James?"

"I have work to do with the lady in Bezetha."

"Mary?"

"Yes, Mary. She is trusting me a little more each time I see her, and I believe that she has something bigger to trust me with when she is ready."

"And you plan to see it through to the end?"

"At least until the timing seems right for a change."

Bat-Ami stood. "It seems that your mind is made up."

"Bat-Ami, please listen. The main reason that I feel I must stay in Jerusalem is what is happening here."

"And what is that?"

"The growth of the church. We are gaining converts everyday. Leaving now would be leaving at the exact time that I should stay. That is why I can't leave now, especially if I were to leave out of fear."

"So you are afraid then?" she said, pointing at him.

"I am," confessed James.

Bat-Ami studied her husband. "I have never heard you say that before. I don't know why, but it makes me feel better to know that you are afraid. I would resent your staying if it was out of stubbornness or defiance of the High Priest. But if you are staying out of obedience, in spite of being afraid, then I will not bring it up again."

James hugged his wife. "Thank you."

She pushed him away playfully. "You can thank me by doing the dishes tonight."

"It will be my pleasure…as long as parsnips are not on the menu."

Bat-Ami turned towards the kitchen. "I do admire your obedience at a time like this, but I pray that it will be worth it."

James followed her. "Blessed is the man who perseveres under trial, because…"

"Because," Bat-Ami interrupted as she finished the expression she had heard many times before, "when he has stood the test, he will receive the crown of life that God has promised to those who love him."

CHAPTER ELEVEN

When tempted, no one should say, "God is tempting me."
For God cannot be tempted by evil, nor does he tempt anyone;
but each one is tempted when, by his own evil desire,
he is dragged away and enticed. Then, after desire has conceived,
it gives birth to sin; and sin, when it is full-grown gives birth to
death.
James 1:13-15

J ames woke the next morning to a loud knocking at his front door. He sat up and quickly looked around the room for Bat-Ami, who was already gone from the room. He lay in bed hoping Bat-Ami would answer the door so he would not have to get up. As he got up he rubbed his eyes, and began putting on his robe. He was almost ready when Bat-Ami entered the room.

"Do you know a man named Symeon?" asked Bat-Ami. "I don't recognize him, but he says that he is a friend of yours."

James stretched. "Symeon is the Rabbi from the Bezetha synagogue."

Bat-Ami nodded in acknowledgement, "He seemed to be relieved that you had not already left." There was a noticeable edge to her voice.

James looked at his wife, aware that there was a question on her mind, but not knowing what it was.

"Are you going somewhere today?" she finally asked out loud.

He spread his hands. "My only plan was to stay here with you and invent a new use for parsnips."

She stepped closer to him. "I'm not in the mood for that, James."

He put his hands in the air. "I have no special plans for today."

"And Ananus?"

"Oh." He turned away from her. "That."

"Yes James, that. Is he here because of Ananus?"

The question startled James. He signaled with one finger for Bat-Ami to wait and he walked around to peer through their bedroom door at Symeon. Symeon was standing at the window looking out. James turned back to his wife and quietly said, "I don't know why he is here, Bat. I really don't."

She tilted her head, waiting for more.

"He may think that I am planning on going to Temple today."

She folded her arms. "And why would he think that?"

James responded, almost proudly, "Rabbi Symeon is exactly like I told you last night. He is filled with raw passion and courage. I told his wife, Isaura that I would be going to Temple soon." He realized immediately how his wife would react to this statement. Looking at her merely confirmed what he already knew. "It is midweek Bat. I always go to Temple at midweek. Besides, if there is political larceny happening in the back chambers at the Temple, then my presence at the Temple may promote guilt or second thoughts."

"Your faith in the goodness of the people is too much right now."

"My faith is not in men, Bat-Ami. My faith is in the Lord our God who wrote His law on the hearts of men."

She breathed deeply. "If you must go to Temple, then going sooner is better than going later."

"I love you, Bat-Ami." He stepped closer to embrace her. "You never cease to amaze me."

She pushed him away. "Just because I know that sooner is better does not mean that I agree with your going." James stepped back. "Just hurry up and get dressed. I'll go see Symeon will be joining us for breakfast." She pointed a warning finger at him. "Hot oats and dates and I'll hear no complaints."

He watched his wife walk from the room. *Who else could be married to me with such grace?*

James and Symeon walked to the Temple in silence. James was quiet. He was always quiet as he approached Temple for prayer. James was surprised that Symeon was quiet too. The young Rabbi usually had something on his mind and he usually put whatever it was to voice.

James looked at the younger man. He knew that Symeon had heard the concerns of Bemus and Adrian, but he did not know how much Symeon might have taken to heart. *It would very much be like Symeon to be here to protect me if he thought that there was a real threat,* James thought. If Symeon had any fear about him, he did not show it.

James found comfort in Symeon's presence. James did not believe that there was a real threat. The Sadducees were too crafty to risk enough aggression to drive The Way underground. Oppression would be a spark that would spread the Gospel rather than stifle it. But still, it took courage to be here with the Bishop at this time. James wondered if the other Jerusalem elders had the same level of courage or conviction as Symeon.

Out of the corner of his eye, Symeon must have caught James studying him. "What is it, Master?"

James put his hand on Symeon's shoulder as they continued to walk. "I am glad that you are here, Symeon."

Symeon's shoulder seemed to lift slightly underneath James' hand.

James spent the rest of the morning praying in the Temple. Normally he would have spent the morning in the Holy Place, but Symeon did not have that privilege. They prayed next to each other in the Sanctuary of the Temple, an area open to all Jews.

As it neared midday, James rose to leave. He noted that Symeon was still on his knees. It was not many who stayed at prayer longer than James. His confidence in the young Rabbi from Bezetha was growing steadily. As he paused over Symeon, James realized that he had not seen Ananus all morning. It was unusual for Ananus to miss being seen at Temple in the morning.

James went to the courtyard in front of the Temple to wait for Symeon. Waiting in the courtyard was a convenient opportunity for James to be seen. If Ananus was already talking about convening a tribunal, James' presence might create some discomfort somewhere.

"Are you James?" The voice that came from behind him was youthful and crisp.

"I am James," James said as he turned to face the young questioner.

The voice had come from a young man of medium height and slender build wearing the formal black robes of a Sadducee priest. The young man had pale skin and dark eyes that did not seem to blink. His voice had a childlike quality but with a caustic edge. "Are you also known as James the Just?"

"I believe I am known by that as well, but I prefer to be called James." James extended his hand towards the young man. "And who might you be?"

James extended hand was ignored. "So James, how did you come to give yourself the title James the Just?"

"He did not give that name to himself; he earned it," sneered Symeon, who had emerged from the Temple and had only heard this question.

"And who are you?" The pale young man sneered back at Symeon.

Symeon's eyes flashed. As he stepped closer to the young man, James placed a hand on his chest.

James noted that the much smaller young man had not retreated, even to break eye contact, with the obviously larger and more rugged Symeon.

"My friend," James said to the pale young man as he kept his palm on Symeon's chest, "you seem to know me. This is my friend, Symeon." Neither man took his eyes from the other. "Now that you know our names, may we know yours?"

"I am Ronen," the young man replied as he shifted his unblinking stare from Symeon to James. "I am a Sadducee, I was trained in Beersheba, and I have been in Jerusalem for a month."

"Ronen—" James nodded— "welcome to Jerusalem. How is it that you know me, Ronen?"

"Ananus is my uncle. He became High Priest two months ago." Ronen's eyes narrowed and his face jutted forward slightly as he added, "You knew that, didn't you, James?"

For reasons that James did not clearly understand, fear clutched at his heart as Ronen identified himself. James knew that he was in danger as surely as if he had been standing before a poisonous snake.

"Yes, of course, I knew Ananus was named High Priest two months ago. Is that why you have come to Jerusalem, to support your uncle?" James asked Ronen, as he reminded himself to breathe.

"I have come to Jerusalem to support the High Priest," Ronen continued. "This is a difficult time in Israel, and the turmoil in Jerusalem does not help."

James swallowed hard, noting for the first time how tight his throat was. "What turmoil in Jerusalem do you speak of?"

122

"The new High Priest must bring stability to the nation, to the Jewish people. The death of Porcius Festus unsettles the Romans and that unsettles the people."

"Surely they are sending a replacement from the Legion," observed Symeon.

"Yes, surely they are, but it has been nearly three months since Festus died, and there has been no news of his successor as of yet. It has us all concerned." Then, tipping his chin towards James, Ronen asked, "Does it not concern you, James?"

James wondered but did not ask Ronen what he was referring to when he said "it has us all concerned." Instead, James looked at Symeon and then at Ronen. "I have been praying, as always, for the safety of Jerusalem since Festus died, but I have not thought much about his replacement. I must confess that I simply assumed his replacement would be rather like him." As he spoke, James became aware that he had not moved his body in several seconds. He noticed how slowly his arms responded to his will to fold them.

"Ah, yes, the prayer life of James the Just. Your reputation among the people of Jerusalem is to be admired."

James simply smiled and kept watching Ronen. The compliment did not feel very complimentary. He decided that folded arms just made breathing more difficult so he lowered them to his side, again noting how slowly his body responded to his direction.

"You enjoy the respect of the Jewish community as well as that of the...what do you call your sect?"

"The Way," James replied.

"I find it interesting, sir," Symeon piped in, "that you know so much about James but do not know the name of The Way."

Ronen slowly turned to face Symeon and then turned back to face James before asking. "I find it interesting that a member of The Way would still be allowed into the Holy Place. You must truly be an unusual man. I have even heard it said of you that you have spent as much time on your knees at the Temple praying for the people, that some call you 'James of the Calloused Knees.'"

"What is it that you want of me, Ronen?" James asked, tiring of the jousting and aware that he needed to keep Symeon clear of whatever peril was unfolding before them.

"Answer a question for me if you please, James."

James made himself breathe before answering, "What is your question?"

"What is the gate of salvation?" asked Ronen.

"The gate of salvation, why, it is the Messiah." answered James. "What else could it be?"

Ronen looked James up and down before breaking back into a smile. "Yes, yes, James. Well spoken." And then to Symeon, "Is he not the most eloquent man?" Back to James, "I can see that you are a man of wisdom."

James said nothing; the flattery was empty. He neither accepted nor acknowledged it.

"You are probably wondering why I sought you out."

"I was wondering," James paused. "What was your reason, Ronen?"

Ronen smiled sardonically. "It will be Passover soon."

"Yes," agreed James.

"Jerusalem will be filled with Jewish people gathered together for the high holidays. We want you to stand on the highest pinnacle of the Temple and persuade the people not to be led astray."

Symeon abruptly turned and squared his shoulders to James. There was astonishment across his face, as if he were pleading with James for a harsh response to Ronen's request. James calmly smiled at Symeon and waited until his enthusiastic young friend relaxed his shoulders. He was aware that his own breathing was also calming at the same time as Symeon's shoulders dropped. He was glad Symeon was there. Turning to Ronen, he said, "I'd be delighted to do that. Thank you for the opportunity."

Ronen smiled smugly. He did not seem to notice that James was watching him as he looked to the Temple balcony for a brief moment. James did not look at the balcony himself because he was certain that Ananus was standing on the balcony, watching the conversation in the courtyard.

Neither Symeon nor James spoke until they were well away from the Temple. When they were a stone's throw from the Western Portico, Symeon grabbed James by the sleeve and stopped him. "What was that?"

"What?"

"That agreement." Symeon motioned towards the Temple over his shoulder with his thumb.

"Oh, that." James sighed. He stared at the Temple for a long moment. "We need to talk, Symeon."

"We need to talk? Are you seriously thinking about—"

James put his hand across Symeon's mouth and, leaning close to him, waited for him to relax his shoulders. "I accepted the opportunity." He lowered his hand, then held his companion by the upper arms. "It is an opportunity to proclaim the Messiah."

Symeon stared at James' smile in disbelief. "It is a trap, James." He shrugged off the older man's hands. "It is a setup. Can't you see that? They will throw you from that tower if you don't say what they want you to say."

"Yes, they will."

James and Symeon's eyes met and locked.

"Wait a moment." Symeon stepped closer to James. "You know...you know that it is a trap!"

James had not thought of this situation as a trap, but that term seemed to fit. He was clearly in danger. It was clearly a trap, but it did not seem real. He was so detached from his feelings and his body that it appeared to him like a drama at the Roman amphitheatre. A trap was set that put the hero in danger; it was simply the author's method of telling the story. He had not accepted that it was his own story he was watching.

"Of course," said James, almost casually.

"Of course?"

"You heard the reference to Deuteronomy, didn't you?"

Symeon looked confused.

James did not wait for an answer. "Do you remember when Ronen made the reference to the people being led astray?"

Symeon nodded.

"Well, that was it. Leading the people astray is an offense punishable by stoning."

Symeon's eyes opened wider. "And stoning means throwing you from a height first."

"That is true," James complimented the young Rabbi.

"No, but that does not honor the Torah. Stoning is not to be done inside a city. From the top of the Temple would be murder."

James smiled. "True, but I do not think that either Ronen or his uncle will worry about those kinds of details."

"How can you smile?" Symeon asked almost angrily.

"I mean no offense, Rabbi. I am just enjoying your insight."

"This isn't about me, James," Symeon said, shaking his head. "They are going to murder you."

"That is a possibility, Symeon." admitted James.

Symeon folded his arms.

"This is political retribution, Symeon. Ananus sent his nephew because he wanted me to know who was behind this and why."

"We already know who is behind this, but do we know why?"

"Actually, Ronen just answered all our questions. I am being targeted personally by Ananus himself."

Symeon waited quietly for James to continue.

"Several years ago, while Ananus held the position of Temple Treasurer, there was a rumor that he was using the Temple Tax money for other purposes." James looked more directly at Symeon. "Have you heard this rumor?"

"I had not heard this rumor before yesterday," Symeon confessed. "But one of the men at your synagogue told me about it. Is it true?"

James looked away. "Whether or not it is true does not matter. What may matter more is whether or not Ananus blames me for it. And if he does blame me, then that is the reason for his retribution."

"How far do you think his need for retribution will go?"

"We know that they are going to ask me to stand on the Temple and address the question of the gate of salvation. Only when that time comes, they will not let me get away with just saying it is the Messiah."

"Oh James," Symeon said with alarm, "they are going to force you to denounce Jesus."

"They are going to try to force me to denounce Jesus," James corrected him.

"Did you know what you were walking into as we walked to the Temple together?"

"I did not know."

"But you knew that it was possible, didn't you?"

"I suppose I did," James said as he turned his right hand over. "I did not think Ananus would do such a thing, but I must admit that I am not surprised."

Symeon rolled his eyes. "No one from the synagogue believed you were really listening to the warnings. We thought you were being . . ."

"Naïve?" James finished his sentence.

"More like blinded."

"No, Symeon, I am not blind to the timing here. Far from it." James looked towards the Temple again, "Ananus might be a bit blind, but I can see why he believes that this is the time for this strategy."

"How do you mean?"

"Ananus apparently believes that he can get me to do what he wants by threatening me."

Symeon nodded.

"The first threat was the reference to the death of Porcius Festus," James said.

"The Roman Procurator?"

"Yes. Ananus knows that he can't execute anyone without the Romans' involvement. But with no Procurator in Jerusalem, he is certainly bolder."

Symeon stared at James with wide eyes.

"Another threat was the way Ronen phrased the question about the gate of salvation and then followed it with the request about encouraging the people not to be led astray."

"You mean that he set it up to be a stoning offense?"

"The reference to "leading people astray" does set it up to be a stoning offense, according to the Torah."

"Are you saying they want to kill you?" Symeon's eyebrows scrunched together.

"I do not think that Ananus wants to kill me. I think that he wants to humiliate me, and he wants to send a message to anyone else who might withhold their support from him."James stroked his beard. "But I do not think that he would hesitate killing me. If Ananus set this trap up this way, then he will definitely go through with it."

"Oh James," Symeon said as he looked away.

"Ananus does not see that God is gathering together more of the Twelve Tribes in Jerusalem this year than He has gathered here in decades." James held Symeon by the shoulders. "Ananus does not see that the death of the Procurator will encourage more of the Twelve

Tribes to return than ever before. Symeon, don't you see? Ananus is giving me the greatest opportunity to proclaim the Good News since that first Passover when the Apostles were still here."

"He is. I see that."

James smiled.

Symeon smiled back, but then, realizing the cost of this opportunity, said, "But James, Ananus will still kill you."

"I will hardly be the first martyr you know."

Symeon shook his head. "But you might be the calmest."

"I am hardly calm, Symeon. Come, let us keep walking. I have much to do."

They walked quietly towards James' synagogue. As they neared it, Symeon broke the silence. "James, did you say that God was gathering the Twelve Tribes?"

"I did."

"Would you say that about whatever happened?"

James tipped his head toward Symeon.

"Let me ask my question a different way. No matter what happens, a man could say 'the Lord our God did that' about it."

"What is your question?"

"What do you think about God intervening in the actions of men?"

"I do not know about everything that happens. I leave that kind of question to the scholars, but I do think that it is wise to watch for when Our Father's hand is clearly at work."

"Do you believe that God has manipulated the circumstances of this season in order for this opportunity to come to you?"

"I think that the Lord our God's sovereignty will not be denied. I think that He provides opportunities at times, and I think that He uses opportunities at other times. The important thing to me is that when I know His will, I must obey His will."

Symeon nodded.

"By the way, Symeon, *manipulated* is a strange term to use about God."

"I know. Maybe I mean tempted. Do you think that God tempted Ananus? And if God did tempt him with this situation, then how could Ananus be blamed? It would not be his fault, would it? It would be like God hardening Pharaoh's heart, would it not?"

James answered, "No one, including Ananus the High Priest, should ever blame God for how they were tempted. God cannot be tempted by evil and He does not tempt us with evil. If Ananus is vulnerable to temptation, it is because his own evil desire entices him, and that is what to blame. And so, if his evil desire does entice him, it will give birth to sin, and sin, when it grows, will give birth to death, and there will be no one to blame but himself."

CHAPTER TWELVE

Don't be deceived, my dear brothers,
Every good and perfect gift is from above,
coming down from the Father of the heavenly lights,
who does not change like shifting shadows.
He chose to give us birth through the word of truth,
that we might be a kind of first-fruits of all he created.
James 1:16-17

After arriving at his synagogue, James excused himself from Symeon and went in to meet with a man that he had been ministering to for several months. An hour later, when James emerged from his study, he was surprised to see that not only was Symeon still sitting at the back of the room, but Mary was there also.

After saying good-bye to his guest, James walked over to them and smiled. "Were you two waiting for me?"

Mary and Symeon looked at each other. Symeon spoke first. "I was on my way home, but I discovered Mary on her way to see you. She did not know where your synagogue was, so naturally I brought her. I thought that I would wait and escort her home."

"I told him that it was unnecessary," Mary said to James. Turning to Symeon she continued, "Really, I will be fine getting home."

"It might be unnecessary, but it is still a gracious offer, Symeon, thank you." James bowed towards Symeon, then addressed Mary. "Were you just visiting our synagogue or were you looking for me?"

"I wanted to speak to you, Bishop, privately, if it is not too much trouble."

Symeon was quick to solve the problem of his presence. "I thought that I could just wait outside and you could talk here. Would that be alright?"

James put his hand on Symeon's shoulder. "I am sure that that would be all right."

As he stood to leave, Symeon whispered, "I would like a brief word with you after you are done talking with Mary."

"That would be fine," James answered as he watched Symeon excuse himself. Then sitting down next to Mary, he waited for her to begin.

"I want to know how you knew what you knew about me," Mary tentatively said.

"Are you speaking about our conversation yesterday?"

Mary nodded.

"Are you asking me how I knew that someone betrayed you in Tiberias?"

Mary nodded again.

James studied her eyes before answering. "The truth is that I did not know as much as I guessed. It was an educated guess, but it was still a guess. I knew that you reacted strongly when I asked you how you came to live in Jerusalem. And then when I was speaking of Job's lament you referred to someone as a 'dog.'"

"Jackal."

"Yes, that's right. It was jackals, not dogs." James grinned. "It does not take much imagination to guess that you had someone in mind when you said that."

Mary looked away.

"I take it that I was correct. Someone in Tiberias did hurt you."

Mary stared at him and simply said, "Yes."

James closed his eyes and breathed deeply. Now that she was ready to trust him, it was his turn to balk. "Mary, before we go further, I have to tell you something."

He sensed her concern immediately. "Let me explain," he interjected. "Several changes have occurred for me since yesterday. I may not be in Jerusalem for much longer."

She looked suspicious.

"I sensed that you were going to confide in me," James explained. "I thought it was only fair for you to know that this might be the last time we can speak together."

James watched Mary's jaw flinch and he wondered if she was close to tears and fighting them off. He did not expect her to react so strongly. "I would love to hear as much of your story as you would care to share, Mary. Maybe knowing that I am leaving could make it easier."

She shrugged. "Maybe." She fidgeted with her shawl and looked at the door. "You are not the first man to be nice to me since my husband died." She chuckled to herself, "You are not even the first Rabbi to be nice to me."

James felt himself flinch as he anticipated what this secret might be. He did not want her to open up so much that he would not have time to help her heal. Then he caught himself and remembered something that he had often said before: "I am not the healer, I am the witness." He had warned her, and now he would have to trust that God would equip her to finish what they were beginning.

"I think I would like to tell you what happened to me in Tiberias, if you would not mind. It is not a long story, really," Mary explained.

James tipped his head to give permission.

"It started after I lost my husband, Evan, and my son, Illias. The Rabbi in Tiberias was kind to me. He visited me regularly and made sure that I had enough to eat. His name was Otniel. I do not think that I could have survived those first few months without his kindness." She lowered her head and began to cry.

James leaned forward and resisted the temptation to touch her, to hug her. He guessed that comforting Mary physically might have been how things went badly for Rabbi Otniel. He at least wanted her to see a kind face when she finally looked up.

When Mary did eventually look up, she said, "He died." It was a struggle to get the words out through her strained breathing, and it triggered another round of tears.

When she finally seemed to calm down, James asked her, "Did you feel that he betrayed you?"

"Not he." Mary looked startled by the question. "Rabbi Otniel did not betray me. Unless you consider dying a betrayal. No, it was not him. It was his wife."

"His wife?" James asked. Mary's story was not unfolding as James had anticipated.

"After her husband died, she accused me of adultery." She looked hard into James' eyes. "It was not true. He was an old man, and he was faithful to his wife. He was just nice to me."

"I take it that other people tended to believe the Rabbi's widow."

Mary's tone shifted abruptly from sad to mad. "The men were afraid to speak to me, afraid of what their wives would say. And the women—some of them had been my neighbors, my friends—stopped talking to me altogether."

"They are the ones you referred to as jackals?" James asked.

"Does the term not fit?"

"There is no question that you have a justification for anger. But anger is an emotion that you must be careful of, because it can create more problems for you."

"I did not have time for anger. I left Tiberias shortly after Otniel died," Mary said in a deeper voice.

"Is that when you came to Jerusalem?"

"Yes. My husband and I had talked about leaving Tiberias before the accident. We had heard that The Way was strong here and open. We wanted that for our son. We would have come then if there had been work for a fisherman here." She looked down. "Coming to

Jerusalem was my only thought once I decided I had to leave Tiberias."

"I am curious, Mary. When we first met and I asked you how you came to Jerusalem, did you think that I had heard from one of the jackals in Tiberias?"

"I do not know...maybe...well, yes. It felt so familiar. That is how it started in Tiberias."

James rubbed his beard. "How what started?"

"A Rabbi from Ammathus came to speak to me. I was summoned to the synagogue. He asked me how I came to be in Tiberias."

"I see, and you thought that I was doing the same thing, didn't you?"

"I did. I thought that people had made assumptions about my relationship with Marcus," said Mary.

"The Roman soldier?"

"Yes, the Roman." Mary rubbed her hands. "What do people have a problem with anyway—that he is a man or that he is Roman?"

James shrugged. "I was not told about an accusation before I met you."

Mary's head flinched back slightly.

James noticed Mary's reaction, "It's true, when Symeon asked me to talk to you; he said that you were fairly new to his synagogue and were having trouble getting connected."

"No one said anything to you about Marcus?" she asked.

"It is true, Mary, the soldier was mentioned, but it was not emphasized, nor was there any wrongdoing implied. Rabbi Symeon wanted to help you, and he may have been concerned about the possibility of an unhealthy relationship, but he did not accuse you of one."

"You mean he was suspicious?"

"I mean that he was concerned. Do not confuse loving confrontation with criticism and judgment. Symeon was concerned about a member of his synagogue, a woman that he did not know very well."

"But there is nothing to confront."

"And no confrontation occurred." James waited for that to sink in before continuing, "Your relationship with Marcus is unusual, and it is unreasonable to expect that no one would notice. Noticing and inquiring about it is not the same as accusing."

Mary shrugged.

"God disciplines those He loves and He expects that we who make up His kingdom would do the same. Can you think of Symeon's involvement as a part of how The Way works? Can you think of his concern as a gift?"

"I would think that a gift would make me feel better."

"And I would think that the best gifts would make you *be* better rather than feel better."

Mary's face softened.

"So what do you say, Mary, can you accept Symeon as your Rabbi? He is an earnest man, and he will work with passion to make all believers all they were created to be. He is a gift to The Way and he can be a gift to you."

Mary did not look convinced as she sat back in her chair.

"I do believe that Rabbi Symeon can be a bull," James observed, "but his passion and directness should not be confused with suspiciousness or judgmental. I think that under his rough exterior is a great heart of compassion."

"I do like the way he teaches. He has a fire about him," Mary offered.

James smiled and patted her on the back of her hand. Then he stood up in the middle of his empty synagogue and in his preaching voice he boomed, "Don't be deceived, my dear brothers. Every good and perfect gift is from above, coming down from the Father of the heavenly lights, who does not change like shifting shadows. He chose to give us birth through the word of truth that we might be a kind of first fruits of all He created."

CHAPTER THIRTEEN

My dear brother(s), take note of this:
Everyone should be quick to listen,
slow to speak and slow to become angry,
for man's anger does not bring about
the righteous life that God desires.
James 1:19-20

Symeon heard James' voice and came in to find James standing in the center of the room pontificating and Mary giggling. Symeon put his hands on his hips and said, "So is this the secret to the great Rabbi's success?"

James laughed. "Yes, Symeon, you have discovered me. As you see, I can evoke laughter whenever I wish." He bowed towards Mary. "And if my sermons do not work, then there is always my dancing." He extended his arms again and completed a slow turn.

Symeon waited until Mary stopped laughing and asked her, "If you would not mind waiting outside for me, I would be honored to walk you home. I just need to have a brief conversation with the Bishop."

Mary stood and turned to leave, but before going through the door, she stopped. "Thank you, Rabbi. I will remember what you have told me." She smiled warmly. "And I wish you well where you are going."

"Thank you, Mary."

When Mary was out of hearing Symeon pointed at her. "She doesn't know?"

"She doesn't need to know, and for that matter, neither does anyone else." James squared his shoulders to the younger man and in a solemn voice added, "Symeon, you know things about this business that you must keep to yourself."

Symeon squared his shoulders up to face James and raised a finger. "This is precisely what I wanted to talk to you about, Bishop."

"Symeon," James said sternly, "you must promise me that what you heard at the Temple this morning will go no further."

"But…"

"No, Symeon, I must insist. This must be kept secret. I will tell who I need to tell, but it is my decision to determine who that is. It is not your decision. Do you agree?"

"I do not agree, but I will do as you wish," Symeon conceded. "But I still wish to be heard on the subject."

"Very well then, my brother, what word do you have for me?"

Symeon pointed over his shoulder at the doorway. "It is about her."

"Mary?"

"Yes Rabbi." Symeon took a deep breath, "I know you well enough to believe that you will go through with this, even to the point of death, if you believe that it is the Lord our God's will for you to do so. But after I left you this afternoon I started thinking that God would not want you to begin a work in someone and not complete it."

"Someone like Mary?"

Symeon glanced at the doorway again, "You must admit that she has responded to you. You have ministered to her in ways that I could not."

"It is true that I have had success with her. Mary has responded to what we have done together. But it is not true to say you could not accomplish the same things."

Symeon frowned, "I am too much of a bull."

"I am serious, Symeon. I have made more than my share of mistakes, and several mistakes with Mary. Everything I have learned from her is borne out of angering or disappointing her. I am sure that even the next Roman Procurator could do that."

Symeon did not appear to be amused by James' levity. "Mary still needs you, Rabbi, and so do I. Does that not factor in to your discernment of God's will?"

"As a matter of fact, it does, Symeon. Tell me something. When you were thinking to yourself that God would not begin a work in Mary without a plan to finish it, was that the moment you ran into her?"

"Yes, it was," Symeon replied enthusiastically. "Is that not a sign?"

"I agree with everything you are saying, even that meeting Mary on the street might be a sign."

James watched Symeon relax his arms and stepped back. He studied Symeon's face for recognition that he was being coy. "I am discerning the signs differently than you intended."

Symeon looked surprised.

"I do not believe that the Lord our God would have me begin a work that He did not intend to finish, but I do not think that it has to be me that sees it to the end. It could her Rabbi."

Symeon flinched back as if he had been hit.

"Did you not think that I would see it that way?" asked James.

Symeon shook his head no.

"When you were thinking about Mary's continued growth, who did she run into on the street?"

"She ran into me. But I am not ready to give her what she needs." argued Symeon.

"But she is ready, and that is the most important thing." James held his hand out and gestured for Symeon to sit down. "As the Proverb of Solomon says, 'A rebuke impresses a man of discernment more than a hundred lashes a fool.'"

"Are you telling me to rebuke her?"

"No, I am telling you that she is a person of discernment and not a fool, therefore she needs…" He waited for Symeon to finish.

"A rebuke rather than a hundred lashes," answered Symeon.

140

"Very good."

"God our Father has placed her as a link between us. I cannot help but think that it may be your calling to finish what I have started." James paused, "Your gifts must be used to be developed."

"According to my wife, rebuking is my specialty. Isaura says that a rebuke from me is never more than a moment away."

"Your passion is one of your greatest gifts, Symeon, but you must learn to temper it at times. And sometimes you may need to completely redirect it. Remember the Proverb 'An anxious heart weighs a man down, but a kind word cheers him up'?"

Symeon nodded. "Is there anything else from Solomon's wisdom that you want me to know?"

"Remember, 'He who answers before listening-that is his folly and his shame.'"

"You should write a book of wisdom, James," encouraged Symeon.

"That is what my wife, Bat-Ami says too." James stood and offered his hand to the younger man. "If I write a book of wisdom, it will have to be very short."

Symeon stood and clasped James' hand. "Thank you, Bishop. Any last words before I go?"

James thought a moment. "Be quick to listen, slow to speak, and slow to become angry, for anger does not bring about the righteous life that God desires."

CHAPTER FOURTEEN

Therefore, get rid of all moral filth and the evil
that is so prevalent and humbly accept
the word planted in you, which can save you.
James 1:21

J ames stood in the doorway of the synagogue and watched Symeon and Mary disappear into the crowded street. He thought, *Symeon, son of Clopas, you do not know it yet, but you will be my successor.* This moment was disturbed by a noise in the room behind him. The noise startled him, because he thought that he was alone.

"You are truly an amazing man, James." It was Nathan.

"Where did you come from?" James asked.

"When I got here you were attending to a man in your study. You did not hear me, so I went into the library and read. Your people kept showing up to see you. You are a very popular man."

"I went to the Temple this morning."

"So I heard," Nathan said as he approached James.

"I expected to see you there."

"Had I known that you were going to pick today to go, I would have been there to receive you. I was sent to the Essene Quarters with some papers from Herod Agrippa."

"How did you discover that I had been to the Temple, then?" asked James.

"On the return from the Essene Quarters, I came by to see you. Bat-Ami told me that you had gone to Temple this morning." Nathan sat down. "I assumed that you would end up here eventually."

James sat next to him. "What did you want to see me about?"

"I knew that the rumors were upsetting to you, and I just wanted to come by and encourage you. I was afraid that you were unduly alarmed." Nathan gestured towards the open room. "After what I heard here today, I would say that I am too late."

"What did you hear, Nathan?" James inquired.

"I heard nothing of your conversations with the man or the woman. But when you started preaching I looked back in. I could not help but hear everything that was said between you and the young Zealot."

"You should have made your presence known, Nathan."

"I agree, James. It's just that the opportunity to do so kept coming and going so quickly that it escaped me." Nathan tightened his eyes. "I am sorry that I did not announce my presence, but I am not sorry that I have heard your concern. James, believe me, you are overreacting to this whole thing, and I am afraid that your young friend's zeal is influencing your reaction."

"You are not concerned for my safety, Nathan?"

Nathan looked down and shook his head slowly. "I cannot believe there is a plot to kill you. It's preposterous. The Romans would never allow it."

"Porcius Festus is dead, Nathan."

"But the Romans are still here, James."

"That's true. But tell me, why do you think that Ananus turned his nephew, Ronen, loose on me?"

"I do not know why Ananus sent his nephew. Perhaps Ananus wanted to give the young man something to do—something that would let him feel that he was part of Temple life," reasoned Nathan.

"You have not yet met Ronen, have you, Nathan?" suggested James.

"I have not. Why do you ask?"

"Because," answered James, "if you had met him, you would know that he is not lacking confidence. On the contrary, he carries himself with an air of entitlement and privilege."

"Those are very strong words, James," Nathan observed. "I had understood that he was a very young man and new to Jerusalem."

"He is young, Nathan, barely twenty, if that. But menace in his demeanor and the veiled threats in his words belie his age. He is a Doeg."

"Doeg?" Nathan asked. "The official in Saul's court?"

"Yes," answered James, "the one who slaughtered Ahimelech and the other priests when the soldiers refused to obey Saul's orders to execute them for helping David."

"Politics." Nathan put both palms face up and shook his head. "Ananus is a politician. He sees the balance of political power in Jerusalem being threatened. His nephew may be his henchman. But Ananus is too shrewd to go as far as you fear. The Pharisees would never allow it. For that matter, neither would any of the other sects."

"I appreciate that, Nathan, and I agree. The other sects would never let Ananus, or any other Sadducee, persecute an innocent Jew in Jerusalem."

"I am relieved to hear you say that, James."

"No, Ananus has no desire to harm me. His intention is to threaten me and then to discredit me."

"Desperate politics executed by a weak politician," offered Nathan.

"Maybe so, Nathan," James said in a more serious tone, "but his threat, I fear, has gone too far for either of us to back down."

"I hope that you are mistaken." Nathan sighed.

James' eyes sharpened and he leaned forward slightly. "I am often mistaken, but let me tell you what Ronen said, and you tell me if I am mistaken this time."

Nathan nodded and opened his arms.

"He wants me to clear up for the people of Jerusalem what the Gate unto Salvation is."

"The Gate unto Salvation?" Nathan asked. "The Messiah?"

Nathan stepped forward, placing a hand on James' shoulder. "He is simply trying to discredit you, James. It is a clever bind really. No matter what you do, you will look bad to one group or another." He removed his hand and turned to step back. "But we are certainly clever enough to find a way to win this. I'll help."

James added, "Ronen said 'lest the people be led astray.'"

"Oh my. That is a grave threat," Nathan said and sat down. "But I do not believe he has the kind of power or political clout that would put your life at risk." He took a breath. "At least I hope not."

"If you don't think that I am at some kind of risk, then why did you stop by this morning? And when you discovered that I had been to the Temple, why did you make a point of seeking me out here?"

Nathan just stared at the Bishop.

James continued, "Why did you come here in so much secrecy? Is your friendship with me a danger to you?"

Nathan took a deep breath and started to speak, but James interrupted him by laying a hand on his shoulder. "You are torn, my friend."

"Maybe that too, but I think that you are torn between your heart and your head."

The Pharisee began to object, but James interrupted him again. "Let me finish, please."

Nathan nodded and leaned further back into his chair.

"Ronen asked me what the gate unto salvation was and I said that it was the Messiah. Do you think that the gate of salvation is the Messiah, Nathan?"

"I do."

"And do you know who the Messiah is, Nathan?"

Nathan looked at him with an expression that screamed, "Please do not say it out loud."

"The Messiah is Jesus, Nathan, and I believe that you know it." James sat back. "Jesus is the one the prophets spoke about. He is the one we have been waiting for, looking for, praying for. He is the one. You know He called Himself the Good Shepherd, and He said that His sheep knew His voice. I believe that somewhere within your heart you know his voice, Nathan, and you are torn because of how much admitting that will disrupt your life."

"James, I believe that you mean well, but it just is not true. I am a Pharisee, a Pharisee of Pharisees. I have served at the Jerusalem Temple for two and a half decades. I was trained by Gamaliel himself. If God were to speak to my heart, it would be confirmed at Temple, but that has not occurred."

"Surely you are not saying that Temple politics reveals God's will to you the way the Angel of the Lord spoke to Elijah, or Abraham, or Isaiah." James held his hands up, "That is certainly not Ananus' position. He is a...what did you call him...a 'politician,' driven by greed for power and wealth. It is his satisfaction for his greed he seeks, not The Lord our God's will."

"Power and wealth are the commodities of the new world, James," offered Nathan.

"Power and wealth are commodities of the created world. In the world to come they will be of little value. They are not evil in themselves, but the greed for them is. The greed for them will tear your heart in two."

"Let me just say, hypothetically, if I did believe in what you say, what would I do?"

James stood up and placed his hands on each side of his old friend's shoulders. He could not tell if the question was sincere or not. "You know the truth, Nathan. In your heart you know it. Put away everything else that can deceive you and accept the truth. It is only the truth that can save you."

CHAPTER FIFTEEN

Do not merely listen to the word,
and so deceive yourselves.
Do what it says.
James 1:22

Bat-Ami was standing in the middle of the room when James reached home. She was holding the ends of her shawl and wrapped each end around her waist. She was stretching the fabric. She did not move as James approached her, nor when he held her close to himself.

"Well?" she said coolly.

James stepped away from her and chose his words carefully. "Ananus is giving me the greatest opportunity to present the Gospel."

"When?" she asked.

"The day after tomorrow. It is just before Passover and the Temple square will be packed."

Bat-Ami shifted her feet but kept her arms folded across her stomach. "Is it a trap?"

James studied his wife's face. He knew that there was no point in delaying or softening the answer. "It is."

Bat-Ami turned her back to him and held her hands over her mouth. This was the moment that he had avoided thinking about all day. He was wise enough to know that when he had nothing to say he should say nothing.

She wiped her eyes and, turning her head, said, "Go get ready for dinner."

"Are you sure you don't want to talk?" James asked.

She turned to face him. Touching his cheek she softly said, "I am going to want to talk, but not now. Let us have dinner now, and then we will talk later. I am asking for one conversation about this, and then I will let it go."

"You have thought this through."

"All day," Bat-Ami said slowly.

"And prayed about it?" he asked.

"All day."

James stood quietly and admired his wife. She was a strong woman with strong opinions. He did not enjoy her strength, but at this moment he could not have thought of anything about her that he did not consider a blessing.

"Go on." She gently pushed him. "Get ready for dinner."

As James placed the last cleaned cup after dinner, he asked, "Are you ready to talk now?"

"It is time." She sat down.

James moved a chair so that he would be sitting directly in front of her. He waited attentively.

"Am I going to be a widow?" she asked finally.

James fought off the temptation to look away. "God could intervene, of course…"

Bat-Ami placed her hand on his forearm and interrupted him. "No theology lessons tonight, please. Am I going to be a widow?"

"Ananus is going to set it up so that if I do not renounce Christ as the Messiah, then I will be guilty of leading the people astray."

Bat-Ami rolled her upper lip across her teeth.

James explained, "That wording, leading the people astray, is, according to the Torah, a stoning offense." Her eyes widened as she took a deep breath. "It is not what I want, Bat. It is what I have to do."

"I would like you to explain that to me," Bat-Ami requested. "How you *have* to make me a widow."

149

"I have to answer this call, Bat. I am not trying to make you a widow. Do you think I want to die?"

Her eyes flared and sharpened. "Do not make this about you. I know that you do not want that part of it. I know, probably better than you do, that it will be hard on you. But right now, this conversation, this is about me, and I will thank you to respect that."

James held his hands up in surrender. "Fair enough. It is a moment in history, a moment that may never come again. The stage is set in Jerusalem for one proclamation that will either move The Way forward or establish the High Priest's control over The Way. It is a pivotal time, Bat. Whether I like it or not I am in the pivotal position."

"And you feel you must obey. Why can't we go away from Jerusalem, James? You have things to say, things no one else can say. What if writing is a calling? What about obeying that? This task before you is worthy, but it will kill you; writing is worthy too, and it will not."

"Bat-Ami, my beloved, if I could chose my life it would be as it is now, here, with you. But it is not mine to choose. The truth is, Ananus has used his office to require this of me, and if I refuse, there would be no safe place for us anywhere in Israel."

Bat-Ami bit at her lower lip and eyed her husband suspiciously. "If we were to flee, we could flee far enough to be beyond the reach of the High Priest. No, my husband, I know better than that. This is not a choice born out of fear."

James inhaled slowly. "No, it is not a matter of fear. It is a matter of obedience."

"You would be forgiven."

James just looked at her and let her sit with her words.

Bat-Ami's shoulders drooped forward and in a much lower voice she said, "I know."

James reached out and took her hands in his. When she looked up he simply smiled.

"Saul, right?" she asked.

"Saul?"

"He is the King who lost favor with God by disobedience and then tried to make up for it with sacrifices. Is he not?"

James smiled. "How did you get to be so wise?"

"I am married to a Rabbi," she replied. They looked at each other for a moment before she asked, "You have to do this?"

James nodded.

"I will say nothing more about leaving Jerusalem. Nothing more except this: please write. If for no other reason, do it for me."

"What would I write?" James asked.

"Write what is on your heart as you are ending your time with the people that you minister to. Write your last instructions to them. If you write that, then I can add those other essays to the end of it for you."

"Very well, Bat, I will do it for you."

"Do you promise?"

"I promise," James said as he leaned forward.

She stood up and kissed his forehead. "Now tell me how I can help you."

"There are several people that I need to tie things up with…"

"Like Leander and Nicholas?" Bat-Ami reminded him of their sons.

This would be the first Passover that Nicholas, the young Rabbi, was returning to Jerusalem and, since it was the first year that Leander, his older brother, had his own home, the brothers had planned to stay together at Leander's home. They would, of course, take Sabat (Sabbath) at Bat-Ami and James' home. Nicholas was to arrive at Leander's home today. That the boys had a place to be and that it was elsewhere in the current circumstances was a blessing, but it did mean that specific arrangements would have to be made.

"I was going to ask if we could break bread with them tomorrow night," James announced.

151

"I have already seen to that," Bat-Ami stated. "Is there anything else I can do?"

James laughed. "You are amazing."

Bat-Ami did not laugh back. "I mean, for you. Is there anything else that I can do for you?"

"Me?" James asked, touching his chest with both hands.

She held his face with her hands. "I know you. You will stay busy with what you need to do and ignore the feelings that must be all over your insides. This will catch up to you, James. And when it does catch up to you, what can I do for you then?"

He moved her hand and kissed her palm. "You can remind me of what I tell my flock when their hearts falter."

"And what is that?"

"Do not merely listen to the word, and deceive yourself. Do what it says."

CHAPTER SIXTEEN

Anyone who listens to the word but does not do what it says
is like a man who looks at his face in a mirror and,
after looking at himself, goes away
and immediately forgets what he looks like.
But the man who looks intently into the perfect law that gives
freedom,
and continues to do this,
not forgetting what he has heard, but doing it—
he will be blessed in what he does.
James 1:23-25

J ames arrived at synagogue unusually early. He was not sure who else would be there and wanted to make sure that he would have enough time to pray alone before anyone came by. He avoided praying at the Temple for the same reason.

After praying, James found the scroll containing the Psalms and went into his office. He knew exactly what he was looking for, The Shepherd's Psalm. He found it on the scroll, but he did not need to read it as he recited it out loud.

"The Lord is my shepherd, I shall not want.
He makes me lie down in green pastures, he leads me beside quiet
waters.
he restores my soul.
He guides me in paths of righteousness for his name's sake.
Even though I walk through the valley of the shadow of death,

I will fear no evil, for you are with me;
Your rod and your staff, they comfort me.
You prepare a table before me in the presence of my enemies.
You anoint my head with oil; my cup overflows.
Surely goodness and love will follow me all the days of my life,
And I will dwell in the house of the Lord forever."

The Shepherd's Psalm had a special place in James' memory, and as he recited it he recalled the first time that he had heard it used for comfort. It was the night of Joseph's death. Their father had been helping set large beams on a bridge three hours' walk north of Nazareth. A beam had slipped from its mooring and fallen on Joseph, who was in the ravine at the time. He died instantly.

It was one of the most desperate nights of James' young life. He was ten and he shared a bed with his eight-year old brother, Jude. They both lay on their stomachs and neither spoke. James listened to the sound of Jude's breathing and fought off his own tears. His oldest brother, Jesus, was suddenly the man of the family at eighteen. Jesus' bed was on the other side of their small room at the back of their home and it was empty while Jesus sat with their mother in the room she had shared with Joseph. James had expected Mary to cry, but if she did, he never heard her. As she tightened his face, he told himself, "Be strong...be strong...I must be strong for Mother."

The silence in the room broke when James heard Jesus' footsteps return. He had convinced himself, *When Jesus returns from Mother's room, I must be quiet. He will be exhausted, He will need sleep.* But Jesus did not get into His own bed when He returned. Instead, He squeezed between James and Jude until the three of them were nestled shoulder to shoulder. Without looking at either of them, Jesus leaned first into Jude and then into James. Each of the younger brothers leaned back against him and they stayed in that position without speaking for several minutes before Jesus began to pray. He prayed first for Joseph, then for Mary, and finally for their family.

After the prayer, Jesus began to recite the Shepherd's Psalm, "The Lord is my shepherd..." By the time He got to "and we will dwell in the house of the Lord forever." both James and Jude were crying. James held his tears as long as he could, but it was no use anymore. Jesus lay between them, and leaning on him, James and Jude wept without shame. They must have slept that way all night because James had no recollection of Jesus leaving their bed, and Jesus could not have moved without waking them.

The Shepherd's Psalm was never the same after that—never failing to bring the comfort he sought or a tear of remembrance. Without realizing it, he leaned his shoulder to his right. It was the direction that he had leaned on Jesus that night in bed. Jesus was his brother, and he could lean on Him anytime he needed. *"But when Jesus needed someone to lean on...."* James began to think. *"Don't do this now, James. The trials of this day are all you can manage right now."*

James wiped a tear from his cheek. As he replaced the scroll in its stand, he reviewed his plan for the day. He had planned to meet with Adrian and Bemus to discuss the matter of his successor. James did not think that either of his advisers expected to become Bishop, but he was also certain that neither man expected that a young Rabbi from the outskirts of town would become the next Bishop either. After the conversation with his advisers, the next task on James' agenda would be to explain his decisions to Symeon. James did not expect either conversation to be easy. Adrian and Bemus would object to Symeon's lack of experience and so would Symeon. Adrian and Bemus would accept James' judgment after a short discussion, but Symeon would need convincing. *And that is one of the reasons that you are my choice, Symeon*, James thought.

The knock at the door startled him. "Rabbi, can we talk?" It was Mary.

"Certainly, Mary. What can I do for you?"

"Please don't do I," she pleaded.

"Don't do what?"

Mary wrung her hands. "I'm talking about the reason that you won't be in Jerusalem anymore."

"Please, come in and sit down." James led the way. After they were both seated, he asked, "Now Mary, tell me what it is that you think is going on with me."

Mary almost looked angry when she spoke. "You are going to make a speech in the Temple Square, and when you are done they are going to kill you." She swallowed hard.

James fought off his frustrations with Symeon as he looked away from Mary and towards the door. He wondered if Symeon had accompanied her to the synagogue. James wanted to unleash his anger at its source. Remembering Mary, however, he slowed his anger down and turned his attention back to her. "I must confess to you that I am a bit taken aback that you seem to know so much of what I had hoped would remain a secret. Have you shared what you know with anyone else?"

"Not a soul." Mary placed her hand over her breast. "Upon my heart, I promise that I spoke of this to no one."

"No one except Rabbi Symeon?"

Mary shrugged. "That is what I meant: no one except Rabbi Symeon."

"Mary, it is imperative that no one find out about this. The Temple Square will be crowded enough with strangers and factions. Rumblings of plots and intrigue will not protect me, but they might trigger a riot."

"I will not say anything to anyone." She paused. "But if you go through with this, then I will be there."

"Please do not do that. It will be hard enough for me, anyway. Having people there that I care about, who I will worry about, will only make it harder. If I am to spend my life for the Gospel, then let me spend it well."

"What about your family? Won't they be there?" asked Mary.

"No, they won't. My wife knows about the threat against me, but she will not be there. My sons will not know."

"Why not?"

"I believe that if my sons knew about the threat, then they would feel obligated to protect me," explained James.

"Are your sons soldiers?"

"No. My oldest son, Leander, is a carpenter and my youngest son, Nicholas, is a Rabbi."

"A Rabbi! You must be proud."

"I am proud. I am proud of both my sons. They have each found that vocation for which they were called and equipped. Nicholas is a Rabbi in Lydda and we are proud of him but no less so than our other son, Leander. He is a good man—steady, strong, faithful. He is a good carpenter, too. He has found his place in God's Kingdom, and he is becoming mature and complete. No parent could want more for their children."

As Mary nodded, her eyes seemed to drift off to a spot over James' right shoulder. James watched her for a moment before interrupting her concentration.

"Mary," he said softly, "what are you thinking about?"

Mary's head flinched back slightly as she remade eye-contact with James, "I am sorry," she stammered, "I was just…"

Noticing that Mary was struggling to finish her statement, "Thinking?" he suggested.

"I was…remembering…how rude I was to you when we first spoke." She hung her head. "When I heard you speak so proudly of both of your sons, I knew that I had gravely misjudged you."

James watched quietly as Mary rubbed her hands together in her lap.

"Throughout most of my life," she began again, "I have been taught to make sure that I followed the Torah and the tradition." She looked up at James. "My mother always said that a woman who did not know her place was lost."

"I have heard other women say that myself," offered James.

Mary placed her hands on her knees and leaned forward. "But what of women who have no place? Are we lost?"

"I do not believe that anyone is ever lost from the grip of the Lord our God," James said calmly. "But if a person could be lost, then it would not be because he had no place."

"What would it be, then?" asked Mary.

"If lost exists, then it is trying to find one's place in the wrong place."

"Wrong place?" Mary repeated as a question.

"I mean our place in God's Kingdom," James explained. "All of God's children have a calling; a role to play, job to do, a gift to share, or some other way that each of us contributes to and fits into God's plan."

"And our call is our place?"

"Yes, and finding your calling is an important task," answered James.

"Finding your calling...is that what you think is the most important task of life?"

"It seems to me that there are three tasks of life. The first is to become who you were created to be, the second is to do what you were created to do, and the third is to be a good steward of the gifts you have been given to accomplish the other two tasks. When we live according to the perfect law, then whatever we do will contribute to at least one of these three tasks."

"I assume that once you understand who you are and what you are supposed to do, then you would not let anything stand in your way of fulfilling it, would you, James?" Mary asked.

"You have got it, Mary," James said.

Mary blushed and sheepishly asked, "Is that why you feel you must go through with this?"

"Yes it is. I must go through with this because it is who I am and what I am supposed to do."

"I wish I had that."

"But you do, Mary, you do. You may not have come to understand it fully yet, but when you do, believe me, you would rather die than surrender any of it."

"And that is how you feel, Rabbi?"

"It is."

"I think that I would be too afraid to do what you are planning on doing."

"Mary, please do not confuse my certainty with bravery. I am afraid. I am more afraid now than I have ever been in my life."

"How are you handling it?"

"I rely on and remind myself of what I know to be true. Today, I am remembering a verse from The Shepherd's Psalm: 'Although I walk through the valley of the shadow of death I will fear no evil, for He is with me.'"

"And that can comfort you when you need it to?"

"Of course it can, but you must remember it and trust its truth enough to believe it."

Mary nodded but continued to lean forward, as if expecting James to say more.

"When you look into the perfect law and trust it enough to obey what it says, then you will also have it for comfort when you need it. This is what freedom is and it can only be found by trusting the truth. It is good that the truth exists somewhere, but it is far better that the truth exists within you. Obedience is how you hold the truth within you, and when you hold it in you, it is there when you need it. Anyone who does not do what the law says is like the man who looks at himself in a mirror and then forgets what he looks like as soon as he turns away."

CHAPTER SEVENTEEN

If anyone considers himself religious
and yet does not keep a tight rein on his tongue,
he deceives himself and his religion is worthless.
James 1:26

"I do not understand." Mary said with a confused look.

"I did not understand it either, Rabbi," Symeon echoed from the doorway.

James raised an eyebrow at Symeon. "I thought that you might be somewhere nearby. How much of our conversation have you heard?"

Symeon walked over to Mary and handed her a cake. "I walked Mary across Jerusalem this morning, but then I left to go get these." He handed James a small brown cake covered with honey and filled with raisins. "This one is for you."

James took a bite of the cake. "This is still warm."

"They were just made. Do you like them?" Symeon asked as he took a bit of his own.

"I like them very much," James said as he took a big lick of honey from across the top of the cake. "When I was about six years old, my mother began to make these every Wednesday morning after my father left for the day. It was my job to take two to the carpentry shop around mid-morning." James chuckled to himself as he took another lick of honey from the cake.

"I always kept Jesus' cake in my right hand and my father's cake in my left. By the time I reached the shop where they worked, I would have licked all of the honey from Jesus' cake. I licked the honey every one of Jesus' cakes every Wednesday that summer, and I was convinced that Jesus had not suspected a thing."

"At the end of that summer, our entire family was at our cousin's wedding. The celebration was very crowded and very festive, and I bumped into my brother Jude, who was eating a honey covered raisin cake and holding another in his hand. Jude held out the extra cake, and with his mouth full, he mumbled, 'Jesus said to give you this.' I took the cake and noticed immediately that the honey had been licked off. When I scowled at Jude, I realized that Jesus was standing behind Jude licking his lips. Jesus roared with laughter and told us to enjoy our cakes. I knew I'd been caught."

James took another bite. "I think it's the honey topping I like the most."

"Good," Symeon said with a crooked grin. "Remember that when you get around to speaking to me again."

James swallowed. "That conversation is coming, Rabbi Symeon. But while you are feeding me, tell me what it is that you do not understand?" Glancing at Mary, he added, "What you both do not understand?"

Mary answered first. "I did not understand what you said about looking in the mirror."

Symeon nodded his agreement.

James finished his last bite. "Maybe it was a more complicated metaphor than it needed to be. I mean we must treat the Torah as if it is the truth, not just an idea. If we do not treat the Torah as if we believe it, then it is like seeing who you are in a mirror and then acting like you are someone else. If you do not put what you know into your heart, mind, and life, then how can you expect to remember it when it matter?"

162

"That makes sense. Well said," explained Symeon.

"How about you, Mary? Does it make sense to you now?" asked James.

Mary was still holding her cake instead of answering. She stood up abruptly and kissed James on the cheek. "I must go." Tears had pooled in the bottoms of her eyes. "I will never forget what you have done for me." She glanced at Symeon and then back at James. "When I came to Jerusalem, I told myself that I would never talk about what happened in Tiberias, but you got me to speak of it. I did not understand the price that I was paying for keeping my secret, but last night I slept peacefully for the first time in a long time. I am in your debt, and I would rather die myself than betray your trust."

She hurried from the room, wiping her eyes.

"She will be fine," countered James. "But why did you burden her with that?"

"I have done what you taught me to do. I listened to her. And I tried to think to myself, *What would James think?* She is a very strong woman. Her faith has been tested by the weakness of others and her faith has remained true."

"She has been disappointed by people she should have been able to trust," added James.

"Yes Rabbi," Symeon said, "including me. I did let idle gossip about her influence me."

"Is that a confession, Rabbi?"

"It is, and it is a confession that I have made to her as well."

"Well done, Symeon. You cannot change what you do not recognize, but when you are willing to recognize the truth about yourself you can change it. Lesser men tell themselves they have nothing to change."

"That would be another reason that it is important to look into that mirror that you spoke about."

163

James smiled. "Maybe it was a better metaphor than I thought." He leaned forward. "I still have not heard why you told Mary my secret, Symeon."

"Mary and I have spoken quite a bit since yesterday. She has taught me much about ministering to people. We were painfully honest, and when she began to question me about what was happening with you, I found myself in a difficult situation." Symeon scratched his chin. "Mary is very persistent and very perceptive. I would have had to lie or be rude to hold her off. And even then, I believe she would have pursued the answers elsewhere." He looked down at his hands. "But the truth is that I wanted her to know. I thought that she deserved the truth, that she could handle the truth, and that she could be trusted with it."

"All great reasons, Symeon, but it was not yours to tell. I cannot fault your judgment now, but it was a risk."

"Am I forgiven?"

"I cannot forgive you, Symeon, if I do not recognize a transgression." James glanced at the door again. He had hoped to speak with Adrian and Bemus before telling Symeon he hoped he would be the next Bishop, but the timing did not appear to be unfolding according to plan. "I am glad that you came by today because I had something else that I wanted to speak to you about."

"What can I do for you, Rabbi?"

"I had planned on talking to Adrian and Bemus this morning about who should Head the Jerusalem Council when I am gone."

Symeon sat up a bit more.

"I am going to tell them to appoint you in my place," James said, watching Symeon closely.

"Me! No, James, please do not do that. I am no politician. Besides," Symeon added, pointing towards the door, "those two bureaucrats would never support me!"

James chuckled, "Politicians? Is that what you think of me, Symeon?"

Symeon seemed to deflate.

"Well?" James waited.

"No sir. I think you are the wisest, most noble man I know. Your reputation with the people is flawless. And it is deserved."

"Is it your opinion of the Council then?"

Symeon shrugged. "The Way could not flourish in Jerusalem without the Council. I am thankful for what it has to do, but I am no scholar or politician. I am an elder, a shepherd. I belong with a flock. Not here with a bunch of . . ." He caught himself.

"You seem to be having a difficult time not saying what you think."

"I am just being honest, Rabbi."

"Just being honest is often nothing more than an excuse for not controlling the tongue," replied James.

"As long as you speak truthfully, what is the virtue in controlling the tongue?"

"The tongue can both praise God and curse men; it can build up or tear down. Your zeal for the truth is what makes you passionate, but untempered by love, the truth can be a weapon of destruction. Speaking the truth in love is how we might build each other and the body of Christ up into maturity."

"I will try, Rabbi."

"I know you will, Symeon. Controlling the tongue is like placing a bit in the mouth of a horse. Your whole being will follow where you let your tongue go."

"I will try hard to control my tongue, but it will be difficult," confessed Symeon.

"Controlling the tongue is impossible to do, but it is absolutely necessary to try."

"Controlling the tongue seems like a much more possible feat than replacing you as Bishop. I do not think anyone could replace you, least of all me."

"That is what I thought when I became Bishop. You are concerned about replacing me. Imagine how I felt replacing Peter. Did you know that Peter spoke in the courtyard once and three thousand people joined The Way? How would you like to live up to that?"

A slightly nervous laugh came from Symeon. "I hope you realize that reminding me of Peter does not make becoming Bishop seem less daunting. Thinking about replacing you was bad enough, and now there is Peter's shadow as well."

James shook his head and smiled. "Symeon, I am surprised at you. You sound like one of the ten spies."

Symeon raised an eyebrow.

"Moses sent out twelve spies to cross over into the Promised Land and scout. Ten spies came back and reported how big the people were and how well defended their cities were. They were convinced that Moses should retreat. Joshua and Caleb also went out and saw how difficult the task would be, but their advice to Moses was quite different. Do you remember, Symeon?" James knew that this was a very familiar story for Symeon, and he knew that Symeon knew what Caleb had simply said: "If God wants us to do this, then we will be able to accomplish it."

Symeon waited for James to stop speaking and solemnly said, "I do not want this task, but I will do it if you think that is what God wants me to do."

"I do think it is your calling, but I do not want you to do it because I think so. I want you to consider it because I think so. And if you prayerfully consider it, and the Lord our God reveals it to you as your calling, then yes, I want you to obey."

"That is a promise I can make," Symeon said firmly.

"Symeon, if you do decide that it is your calling, you will have to learn to appreciate the gifts of men like Adrian and Bemus. I know that they are isolated from the people they serve and that they can seem detached and indifferent at times, but you must remember that the Body of Christ has many different parts and each must do its job. Adrian and Bemus have an important part to play. As head of the Council, you will have to learn to consider them as your flock too."

"I had not thought of that," observed Symeon.

"Clear and loving thinking is how the tongue is controlled."

Symeon nodded acknowledgment. "Controlling the tongue is a very important principle."

"If anyone considers himself religious," James said, "and yet does not keep a tight rein on his tongue, he deceives himself and his religion is worthless."

CHAPTER EIGHTEEN

Religion that God our Father accepts
as pure and faultless is this:
to look after widows and orphans in their distress.
James 1:27

"Have you two got it all settled?" Bemus asked as he entered the synagogue.

"Have we got all what settled?" asked James.

"Whatever it was that you were debating," Bemus explained. "When I walked in, it looked to me like you had just reached an agreement. Am I mistaken?"

Symeon looked to James. "I thought that he did not know."

James sighed; he knew what would come next.

"What is it that I don't know?" Bemus asked excitedly as he came closer to them.

"Please gentlemen, let us sit." James gestured towards a cluster of chairs.

"Bemus did not know," James explained to Symeon as they seated themselves, "but he does have exceptional skills in finding out whatever there is to be known."

"What kinds of things?" Symeon asked.

"Anything," Bemus shrugged.

"Everything," answered James.

Bemus smiled at James.

"I suppose that I must explain now that you have asked." James recapped the encounter in the Temple courtyard from earlier in the day.

Bemus' head slowly dropped as James spoke so that by the time James repeated Ronen's threat, Bemus was squarely facing the floor in front of his feet. He did not lift up his head until after James had finished speaking. When he did finally lift his head he sat facing James and stared hard into James' eyes. His face was slightly red as he stated, "I am sure you know what this means."

"It means that I will be expected to denounce The Lord Jesus Christ in front of a host of the Twelve Tribes in the Temple Courtyard."

Bemus looked from James to Symeon and back to James. "And what do you think they will do when they discover that you won't cooperate with their plan?"

"My plan was to speak to you and Adrian first this morning and then, depending on that conversation, proceed from there."

Bemus placed his hands on his knees and leaned forward as far as he could. He scowled at James. "That does not answer my question."

"I have told Rabbi Symeon that I plan to recommend that the Jerusalem Council appoint him as Bishop."

Bemus turned quickly and faced Symeon where he sat. "You and James have spoken of this then?"

Symeon nodded.

"And I suppose there is no use in discussing options." Bemus said, still facing Symeon.

James cleared his throat and waited until both Bemus and Symeon were looking at him, "As far as responding to Ronen's threat there are no options. But if you are speaking of options about who is to become the next Bishop, then a discussion may be in order. What did you have in mind, Bemus?"

Bemus stood up and with both hands on his heart he said, "I meant no disrespect against you, Rabbi Symeon. The threat against the

169

Bishop was all I had on my mind." Then, extending his hand, he moved to stand in front of Symeon. "If a successor must be named, then I think you are an excellent choice."

Symeon looked overwhelmed as he grasped Bemus' hand.

James intervened. "Please, Bemus, you are smothering him."

Bemus took a step back. "I am sorry. I did not know, but you have my full support, really."

"I can see that, and I thank you, but I do not know why," confessed Symeon.

Symeon looked at James, but James just smiled.

"Do we...know each other?" Symeon asked.

"We have spoken casually at Council meetings and at Temple. I was there when you were commissioned to Bezetha. So no, we do not really know each other, but there is not a Rabbi around Jerusalem that I do not know about."

"If you do not mind, brother Bemus, I am curious as to what you know about me."

Bemus looked to James for direction.

"If you have some thoughts about our brother, share them with him," James encouraged.

"Very well." Turning to face Symeon, Bemus reported, "My understanding is that you are an insightful, but unpolished teacher. My impression is that people who hear you believe you."

Symeon smiled awkwardly.

"It is said that you have the zeal of a Zealot and would have made a great assassin if it were not for your sense of duty." Bemus hesitated and looked at James. "It is also said that you sound like a young James the Just."

Symeon blushed.

James laughed.

"My delight in hearing that you will be Bishop is—"

James interrupted. "It is not settled, Bemus. It is merely my recommendation. I do not want to mislead Symeon."

Rolling his eyes, Bemus turned to Symeon. "If James recommends it, it will be. Mark my words. My delight is not so much about my knowledge of you, Rabbi, although I am quite comfortable with what I know. My delight is in the fact that James has a recommendation, and to a man, the Jerusalem Council will trust his judgment." Turning to James he added, "If you had not left an opinion, then my fear was that it would have been Adrian."

James grinned, "And that would have made life very difficult for you. Is that not true, Bemus?"

"It is most definitely true," Bemus agreed, then explained to Symeon, "Adrian and I love and respect each other, but we are very different. We are both advisers to the Bishop. We are not leaders, we are not teachers, and we are not Bishop material. Our benefit to the Bishop is that we are different from each other and different from him."

"Bemus' skill at acquiring information is related to his ability to...how shall I say this, Bemus?"

"Bend the rules?" Bemus suggested.

"Thank you Bemus, that was well said." James nodded towards his adviser.

"I can bend the rules without breaking them," Bemus proudly admitted. "But my friend Adrian has never bent a rule in his life and he cringes when I do. If he became Bishop, then one of use would wither and die within a season."

"And why would you dread being Bishop yourself?" asked Symeon.

"Oh please." Bemus laughed. "That would make me old faster than if Adrian were Bishop. No, I have found my calling, and it is not Bishop. The next Bishop has got to be a teacher and a leader. The next Bishop should be a man like you, Symeon. And a man like you will need advisers like Adrian and myself. When the time comes, you will have the same loyalty from both of us that we have always given to James."

"Thank you for that," James said to Bemus. "I would have expected nothing less."

"I thank you for that, too," Symeon said, "but I do not know what else to say. This is all a bit overwhelming for me right now. I think that it is time for me to return to Bezetha." Symeon stood up. "I want to go to the Temple alone and pray for a while."

"That is what you should do then, Symeon." James was comforted by how the two men had responded to one another.

"Bishop Symeon," Adrian announced from the door of James' study.

Adrian's voice startled James. He had a scroll open before him on the desk. He was reading about the destruction of the Temple that Solomon built.

"I see that you have already been informed." James pushed away from his reading. "I had wanted to tell you myself. Forgive me."

"Oh James, think nothing of that. Bemus was here ahead of me." Adrian shrugged. "There would have been no way to keep it from him. He is a ferret."

"He *is* a ferret," James agreed. "What do you think about my recommendation?"

"I do not think that there is another choice," Adrian analyzed. "I am concerned about his age and experience. Symeon is relatively unknown and his experience consists of a one-year long appointment to the poorest and least influential synagogue in all of Jerusalem. His appointment will come as a shock to many."

"That is a good insight, Adrian," James complimented his adviser. "Are there any other concerns that you can foresee?"

"It will be difficult for anyone to replace you, James." Adrian's eyes glazed and looked down.

James reached out and held Adrian's elbow. "I trust that you will find the way to protect him from unfair comparisons."

"I think that we should wait at least six months before appointing him," Adrian said as he regained his composure. "It will still be hard for him, but six months will at least give him a fair start."

"Well done. I knew that you would know what needed to be done."

Adrian smiled. As James began rolling up the scroll on his desk, Adrian asked, "What were you studying, James?"

James cradled the scroll in his arms, "I had never noticed this before, but when Nebuchadnezzar destroyed Solomon's Temple and carried the people off to Babylon, he made them into servants."

Adrian looked confused.

"We are all servants, Adrian, but when the people forgot that they served the Living God, they became servants of something else."

"That sounds like something you would notice, James."

James, Bemus and Adrian ate their noon meal together, sharing appreciations, regrets, and good-byes. When they arrived back at the synagogue, Nathan was waiting in the office. Adrian and Bemus excused themselves and left together.

"I did not expect to see you today, Nathan. I thought you were leaving for Jericho today."

"I am. I wanted to see you before I left."

"What brings you back to my synagogue, Nathan?"

"I did not sleep well last night."

"I hope that it was not because of something I said," James offered.

"Neither of us believes that, James. You said things to me that you hoped would disturb me."

"True, I had hoped. I still hope that you will come to know the truth, and that it will lead you to freedom and life. But I meant it when I said that I did not desire for you to be disturbed."

Nathan pulled on his ear. "But if I come to accept what you think is true, then a few nights of disturbed sleep is fine with you. Is it not?"

James extended his hands forward and mimicked a scale. "Let me see—" he moved his hands up and down as if weighing his answer— "a few nights versus eternity. Yes, I believe that I would be fine with that exchange."

"I suspected as much, you old schemer," Nathan said as he playfully slapped at James' shoulder.

"Did my *scheme* work?" asked James playfully.

"Do you mean, am I ready to profess Jesus as the Messiah?" Nathan asked.

"Are you?"

"No. There are still too many questions for me."

"Then can I provide an answer?" James offered.

"I'm not sure. I have considered whether or not Jesus could be the Messiah, and I conclude that it is impossible." He waited for James to react, but James did not. "Then, as I realized that God becoming a man was impossible, I also realized that being impossible would not stand in His way."

James smiled slightly.

"In fact, believing the impossible is what would get in the way of men. That would make believing impossible."

James tried to encourage Nathan to continue with only his expression and body language.

"Then I asked myself, 'Why would God make believing impossible?'"

"And how did you answer your question?" asked James.

"If Jesus is the gate, then we must enter by way of faith, not reason," answered Nathan. "Is that how you would answer that question, James?"

"It is. Your heart is very close. Why do you resist?"

"I am open, James, but not convinced. I still have questions about what it means in my life right now. If I accept that Jesus is the gate unto salvation, then my whole life has been misguided. I have been a Pharisee, a servant of God and His people, but I have not only been misled, I have misled others. How can I not question what you believe?"

"You must do the good you know to do, my brother. Anything else is sin. You have been faithful to what you knew and now you know more. The God you have served is still God, knowing Him more now does not change Him. The work you have done, teaching the Torah, preaching faithfulness—these have all been good works and need no defense. But if you continue to deny the truth that you know then your heart will harden." James looked to the stand where he had place the Psalms scroll earlier. "It would be like the first Psalm."

"You mean, 'walking in the counsel of the wicked, standing in the way of sinners, and sitting in the seat of mockers'?"

"Yes. The problem with denying what you know to be true is that you have to believe a lie, and lies will not stay still. If you believe a lie, then you will have to work harder and harder to continue to believe it."

Nathan bowed towards James. "You are Rabbi of Rabbis."

"And you are close to the Kingdom of Heaven," responded James.

"Tell me, James, besides believing, what would you encourage me to do? How might I be a religious man?"

James pondered for a moment. *This is a man who knows the Torah, who leads a contemplative life of study and scholarship.* James thought about repeating the famous anecdote about Hillel, who was asked if he could teach the entire Torah while standing on one foot. The story has Hillel responding with the phrase "Do unto others as you would have them do unto you. That is the entire teaching of the Torah. The rest is just commentary."

Realizing that Nathan would surely know the Hillel story James decided to say something of his own. James placed his hand on his old friend's head. "My prayer for you is that you accept the word that is planted in you. But until then, and after then, I remind you of what the prophets all knew." James paused. "Your faith will never be pleasing to God, our Father, if in your piety you forget the widows and orphans in their distress."

CHAPTER NINETEEN

*...and to keep oneself
from being polluted by the world.*
James 1:27b

James stood in the doorway of his bedroom and watched Bat-Ami sleep. Time slowed down while he watched her chest rise and fall as she breathed. He felt himself nearing tears. The warmth began in his neck and crept up towards the back of his eyes. His chin began to tremble. The only thing that kept his tears from flowing was concentrating on his own breathing, and that would not have worked for long, but he heard Bat-Ami speak.

"Are the boys gone?" she asked.

Leander and Nicholas had spent the evening with Bat and James. Bat-Ami had arranged for their children to come to dinner. It gave James the opportunity to say good-bye to his sons. James and Bat-Ami agreed that they could not tell Leander and Nicholas what was about to happen. The boys would have felt compelled to die at their father's side.

Bat-Ami suggested that instead of going to the Temple square the next day, she would keep the boys with her at Leander's home. Nicholas, the Rabbi, was in Jerusalem for Passover staying with Leander.

"They just left." James put the candle he was holding on a chair near his side of their bed. He put his nightshirt on and climbed into bed next to his wife.

"What did you tell them?"

"I told them that I was proud of them." The sadness was heavy in his throat. He could not swallow, and he felt even warmer as the first tear rolled down his cheek.

Bat-Ami put her arms around him and pulled him closer to her. She held him there, his head buried against her neck, while he wept.

How long they lay like that James did not know. She let him cry until he was done. When his breathing was back under control, he pulled his head back far enough to kiss her tenderly. He could taste sale on her lips.

"I can't imagine being married to anyone else," he said softly as he moved a few strands of hair from her face.

"I should hope not."

He smiled. "I mean it. You have allowed me to pursue the business of my life without ever putting pressure on me to do anything different."

He watched her eyes move from one of his to the other. "You have been the perfect wife, Bat."

Touching his lips with her fingertips she said, "Not perfect."

"I love you."

"I love you, too."

James slid his arm under Bat-Ami's head and kissed her again. As they broke apart, they both shifted. James found himself on his back with his wife's shoulder nestled under his arm and her head on his chest. He stroked her hair.

Whispering he said, "Thank you for the last few days."

Bat-Ami lifted her head and stroked his chest.

"You deserved every moment of my time these last few days. I wish I could have given it all to you."

"I know," she said as she put her head back down on his chest.

"I have thanked God every day of our life together that He blessed me with you, but I have not realized until now how much I have depended upon you." He started stroking her hair again. "I count on you all the time and you have never let me down, even tonight."

"What do you mean?" she asked without lifting her head from his chest.

"You arranged this time with the boys, and then you left us alone. You know, Bat, it would have been fine for you to have stayed with us."

"I know it would have been fine. I just don't think that I could have."

James could feel the warmth wash over his face again. He lay still and slowed his breathing.

"You have been the best husband. You are my whole life, James." She lifted her head and watched his eyes turn red and glossy. "Can I at least tell you that I love you with all my heart and soul?"

James could not speak. All he could do was inhale deeply and widen his eyes.

Bat-Ami bit her lip. "I won't say any more. You know how I feel."

Still unable to speak James nodded yes.

"Are you still going to try and write tonight?"

He took two deep breaths before answering. "I know you want me to. I'm just not sure what to say."

"Maybe it would help if you thought about who you are writing to while you are writing. I'm sure it will come to you once you get started."

"I'll try, Bat."

"Writing to the people of God is really no different than what you have done these last days. Just remember what you have been saying to everyone as you said good-bye. Surely your conversations with Nathan, Mary, Symeon, and even me are full of inspiration. Use that. What were your last words to Nathan?"

"We spoke about the difference between faith and religion. I told him that his piety would never be pleasing to God if he forgets the widows and orphans," answered James.

"Really, you said that?"

"I did, why?"

"I thought that you would have talked to Nathan about the Lord. Do you know if he has made his peace with the Messiah?" asked Bat-Ami.

"We did talk about the Messiah. He sounded like he was close, but I do not know." James rubbed his eyes. "Who but God knows anyway? What I know is that Nathan knows what he needs to know. He is a good man and I hope the Lord softens his heart. But until that time arrives his religion is important to him."

"So you told him to care for widows."

"Of course. That's what religion is: applying your faith to your life. Do you disagree?"

"You know I don't disagree. I just think that most of the time if someone asked you what religion was then you'd say something about being true to yourself or overcoming the pollution of the world."

James looked off. "That's good too. I wish I had added that. Say, I have an idea, why don't you write it?"

Bat-Ami smiled. "Don't think that I didn't think about it. I think it would be easier to write it myself than to get you to do it."

James shrugged.

"Even if the people would accept it from a woman, I'd still just be repeating my husband's ideas."

"The ideas that your husband learned from his wife, you mean."

"Go write, James," she said as she lay back down on her side.

James lay back down on his side facing Bat-Ami. "I will, I promise."

Bat-Ami rolled on her back and gently stroked his cheek. "You know, James, you have kept yourself from being polluted more than any man I know."

"Some would say that I am just stubborn and independent."

"And they would be right, but beyond that you never let the opinions of the wealthy and the powerful keep you from doing what you thought was right."

"Maybe it would have been a wise thing to have done a few times," James wondered.

"Stop it. You don't think that for a minute."

"No, I have had many minutes that I thought that way. You give me too much credit, Bat."

"No I don't. You may have had thoughts of selling yourself, but you never did. I am, and have always been; proud of the way you live your life. I wouldn't ask you to change any of it."

"Even now, Bat?"

"I wish I could change it. If I could I would. I have prayed every day that God would change Ananus' heart. I have even prayed that God would strike him down."

"Bat!" James exclaimed.

"I know, James. I'm just being honest."

He reached out and stroked her cheek.

She held his hand. "But I have never asked you to be different or prayed for you to be different." She turned her head away from him. "I know that it would kill you to be anything other than what God has called and equipped you to be. I know that you'd rather die than compromise yourself. That's why I'd never ask for you to do anything different." She turned back. "That's why I'd never want anything different. Even now."

James kissed her and then they lay together without speaking. He held her against his side with her head resting on his chest again. When she finally sounded like she was asleep, he eased his arm out from under her head and got out of bed.

181

✝

The lamp on the table seemed to flicker unusually as James sat, pen in hand, staring at the blank parchment before him. He had expected starting to write would be easy because he had been collecting thoughts for several days. He had followed Bat-Ami's idea to keep a memory record of his last words to the important people he had spoke with over the last few days, but many of the thoughts that were clear to him earlier were escaping him now. As he watched the flame dance he found his thoughts drifting to the past.

A new memory came into view...one he had long forgotten. He was six and his family had made the trip to Jerusalem for Passover. It was the first time that he had come to Jerusalem for the high festivals; he had not wanted to come. His younger brothers, Jude and Joseph, got to stay in Nazareth. He had wanted to stay at home, too, and he had been quite boorish about saying so. The entourage of uncles, cousins, and neighbors from Nazareth had been too large to be housed all together, so they all stayed in different homes throughout the city. James stayed with Jesus in the upper room of the home next to the home of Obadiah the merchant where their parents stayed. When the day came to leave Jerusalem, Jesus had hurried off for one last time at the Temple before leaving for home.

"Tell Father and Mother I went back to the Temple," Jesus said to James as He woke him up that morning. "I left some fresh water for you on the table. Don't forget to bring the pitcher down with you when you get up. Come get me if they decide to leave early."

James agreed to do what Jesus had asked and then went back to sleep. It was mid-morning when Obadiah's son, Quentin, came to get the two brothers because the entire Nazareth caravan was ready to leave. James scrambled down the back stairs, ran past the back of line of older kids, and joined his parents in the middle of the caravan. It was not until they passed through the gates of Jerusalem that James remembered he had forgotten what his brother had told him.

The chill James felt sitting before the flickering flame was not unlike the chill he had felt when he realized his brother was not with them. He knew he should find his parents and tell them. But the frustration he felt about the prospect of stopping the journey back to Nazareth was quickly replaced by embarrassment that he had forgotten something so important, and this feeling settled finally into anger at his parents for making him come and at Jesus for putting him in such an embarrassing position. So James did nothing.

Eventually Mary noticed that her eldest son was missing. The caravan was only an hour's walk from Jerusalem by then, so it was agreed that all could wait for Mary and Joseph, along with three of the other men, to return to the city for Jesus. James was not invited to go with them so he waited with the others for their return. It was early afternoon when they returned, but the wait seemed much longer to James, for he knew the truth would become known as soon as they asked Jesus to account for His absence.

The moment of truth never came. When the first of the group returned from the search for Jesus, they reported, "He was at Temple, and when Mary scolded him He said, 'Did you not know that I would be at my Fathers' house?'"

But James had not laughed. He was sick to his stomach with anticipation. It was not the punishment from Joseph that he dreaded or the scolding from Mary. It was the look of disappointment in his brother's eyes that he most feared. When Jesus first rejoined the group, he stayed at the back of the caravan with the other kids his age. James could do nothing but walk alongside Joseph and wait for the moment of reckoning to come.

James sighed. The memory was fresh to him and it would certainly have brought a tear to his eye if he had not already cried so much that night. He recalled being startled as his brother suddenly appeared next to him as they walked. He had not seen Jesus approach, but he felt Jesus' arm around his shoulder and his voice whispering in his ear, "Did you forget to return the pitcher too, Jamie?" Then Jesus laughed and kissed him on the forehead. "Don't look so serious, brother."

James realized then that he had not thought of this moment since he was six, which led him to admit, "He never told. Jesus never told." James' next awareness was that he himself had never told either. He let his brother bear the consequences of his forgetfulness. His mouth was thick, sticky, but he could not swallow, so he put the pen down and got up from the table to get a drink. He wanted to cry again but could not. Maybe it was all of the tears he had already cried that night, maybe it was exhaustion, or maybe it was the weight of what he faced in the morning. Whatever it was, tears escaped him as he sat back down.

James hoped that picking up the pen and touching it to the page would get the writing started. He deliberately avoided looking at the flame. But his mind was still blank and eventually another unsolicited memory came forward. Instead of the old familiar regrets that had often intruded into James' thoughts, the picture of his last conversation with Jesus appeared in his mind as he was once again mesmerized by the flame. It was a conversation that occurred after Jesus had been crucified. Jesus had appeared to many of the faithful after His crucifixion and resurrection. His glorified appearance after the resurrection was not simply an encouragement to the Apostles and a testimony to the Messiah's victory over death. *It was also an opportunity to speak to His brothers,* James realized, *I was the last person Jesus appeared to...the last person He had a personal conversation with before He gave the Great Commission to the*

184

multitude and then ascended to heaven. It was as if Jesus could not go until He saw His brother. With that thought, James put down the pen and laying his head upon his crossed arms, he began to weep.

Weeping did not slow the memories down. Before he realized it, James was remembering being twenty-seven again and standing on the roof of John's Jerusalem home. It had been five weeks since Jesus was crucified. Mary had come home with John that day and had been there since. James, Jude, and Simon, had come several days later to get their mother. Their plan was to bring her back to Nazareth, but she would have none of that. They had expected her to be distraught with grief, and she surely was, but she was strangely peaceful too. The tenor of the people she associated with, all of whom were followers of Jesus, was a mixture of grief, some disillusionment, and mostly fear. Mary was neither disillusioned nor afraid. "I belong here now," she told her sons, "they need my peace."

After a few days, it was agreed that Simon and Jude would return to Nazareth. The carpentry shop, Joseph's carpentry shop, needed tending. Although it made much more sense for Jude, the only unmarried surviving brother, to have stayed in Jerusalem with their mother, James insisted that it was his responsibility.

"I will be fine," Mary had told him. "Go home to Bat. I will come when the time is right." Then she had held his face in both her hands. "Please do not feel bad, my son, but try to understand."

Mary's words, "try to understand," were as close to evangelizing about the Messiah as she ever spoke to him. It was just like her, he realized, to say exactly the right thing and then to leave her words alone to do their work on him.

But he could not bring himself to even consider leaving his mother.

As Simon and Jude prepared to return to Nazareth they begged James to reconsider. "Is it guilt?" each had asked.

"I have to stay here in Jerusalem," James told his brothers. "I do not understand it, but I know it is not my guilt that holds me here. It is my responsibility." James knew that when Jude and Simon left Jerusalem neither of them agreed or understood why he had been the one to say.

For a month, James was treated as an honored guest in John's home. He had tried to visit the Temple during the day, but the conversation about his brother made him uncomfortable so he spent his days either walking through the city or accompanying Mary to the market. When they were in the open in Jerusalem, Jesus' name was never mentioned. In John's home, however, there was rarely any topic of conversation other than Jesus. Visitors, mostly those who had been with Jesus or had followed him, came every evening, telling stories of what they had seen or heard. James listened to them talk. It was clearly his brother that they spoke of, but James did not recognize Him. Yet he grew more and more curious about their stories.

At first James thought they were merely misguided as he listened to them speak as if his brother was God. But when he heard them say that Jesus had made the claim Himself, James wanted to lash out at them in anger. He could not believe that his brother would speak what his Hillel training told him was blasphemy. He held his tongue when he looked at his mother. Mary was there. She knew what Jesus had said and what he had not said, but she made no objection to their claim. Mary had just smiled at him as she watched him take it all in.

Confusion was the only way to describe what James felt. As he came to know, in intimate detail, the stories of the last three years of his brother's life, James became more confused. This was Jesus, his brother—the one he played with, played tricks on, was jealous of, looked up to, competed with, learned from, admired, loved, and...yes, betrayed. How could He be the Messiah? John had spoken of Jesus appearing to the Apostles a few days after He was crucified. James had heard that story many times. John was such a nice gentle man, and he obviously loved Jesus, so James always took the story to be figurative, symbolic. "Surely He did not *really* appear to them after He died," James told himself each time he had heard the tale.

It is just figurative, he had thought each time he heard the tale until one night. This night he realized that John literally believed Jesus had appeared before them in some sort of glorified angelic body. *Could it be true? Is Jesus the Messiah? Is my brother, Jesus the carpenter, The Lord?* The question, in every imaginable form, swarmed through his thoughts as he stood alone on John's roof staring into the night sky. All the visitors had left and everyone else had been asleep for hours, but James stood there, wide awake, on the edge of John's roof. He did not notice that his knees were leaning against the four-foot wall that lined the roof. If that wall had given in, he would have fallen face-first from the roof. And in that, almost prayerful posture, the answer to his question became clear to him. As he realized the truth, he uttered it out loud to the heavens: "You are the Messiah. My dear sweet brother, you are truly the Messiah."

The excitement that lifted his voice passed quickly, and again his utterance was out loud, only this time it was a whisper. "I am so sorry, but I did not know. I have always loved you...but I did not know."

James' next instinct was to go and wake Mary. He wanted to tell her that he understood. But when he turned from the wall, he could not move forward because standing directly in front of him was his brother. It was Jesus all right. He looked different, but there was no mistaking it; it was Him.

He was looking, really looking, into Jesus' eyes. Moving was out of the question as he watched Jesus take a step forward and lean even closer. Jesus' eyes went back and forth from James' right eye to his left. Nothing needed to be said aloud for James to find complete acceptance in Jesus' eyes. James never doubted his place in the Messiah's Kingdom. All James could do was let his brother hold him while he cried.

James remembered Bat-Ami commenting often on his "unshakable confidence." It was an observation he would always dismiss saying, "I am not really confident, I just seem confident when the right thing to do is clear." But he realized, sitting there alone, he was not just clear, he was confident, and now he knew why.

His weeping slowed enough for James to lift his head and take a deep breath. As he listened to his breath leave his mouth, a new thought occurred to him. *My recognition that the Messiah was my brother came at precisely the moment the Messiah ordained it to come.*

Another wave of tears came. Deep, from the belly tears, the same kind of tears he had cried that night on John's roof. James' nagging regret was not in failing the Messiah; he knew he, like everyone, had failed the Messiah. He knew that he had been forgiven for that. The nagging regret James felt was that when Jesus needed him the most, he had failed his brother. The fact that he had failed his brother, the brother he loved, at his moment of most need was the painful regret that had haunted James for so long that he was not surprised when it once again crossed his mind.

"I'm sorry,' he whispered, collecting himself.

As James looked at the flame, once more the memory of that night continued. In his mind's eye he saw the Messiah's face leaning close to look deeply into James' eyes. As his brother held him, the Messiah whispered in his ears, "Oh that all men would love me like you do." After that James was alone again on the roof. His brother, the Messiah, was gone.

James wept again. He wept as if he were hearing Jesus' words of assurance for the first time: "Oh that all men would love me like you do."

He was vaguely aware that his eyes were tired when he finally lifted his head, but mostly James felt peaceful. There was no way to tell how long he had been thinking, but he knew he had some things to write and he was ready. Before writing anything down, James reminded himself again of what Bat-Ami had said: "Just write down the things that you have been saying to people these last few days." He began writing:

James, a servant of God and the Lord Jesus Christ,
To the twelve tribes scattered among the nations: Greetings.

Before he wrote more, his thoughts wandered to how he would end. He decided to end with what he had told Nathan about religion: "*Religion that God our Father accepts as pure and faultless is this: to look after widows and orphans in their distress.*"

"But," he said out loud, "what was it that Bat-Ami wanted me to add to that?" Then, answering his own question, he said, "*and to keep oneself from being polluted by the world.*"

CHAPTER TWENTY

What good is it, my brothers, if a man claims to have faith
But has no deeds? Can such a faith save him?
James 2: 14

The entire day had been filled with dread. Bat-Ami was resigned that a knock on the door was coming, and that with it would come the news of James' death. It was beyond belief for her that neither of her sons had noticed her detached and distracted mood. It was also possible they had, but had no idea how to ask her about it.

Bat-Ami was not surprised that Nicholas had not noticed her mood. Nicholas was the younger son, the Rabbi. He had always been the more analytical of their sons. His approach to his rabbinic duties was to teach the Torah, which he had been hungry to know since he was a small boy. Nicholas had inherited James' tendency to get lost in his own thoughts. If he had missed Bat-Ami's mood, it was likely he was thinking about his next sermon or a debate with a Pharisee.

But Bat-Ami expected Leander to notice. He was older and had always been the more sensitive of the two. If this were not an especially busy workday for Leander, the carpenter, Bat-Ami would probably not have kept her secret.

The day had begun for Bat-Ami when she finally awoke from the strained few hours of sleep that she had managed after listening to James work in the other room for most of the night. She did not remember going to sleep, and the memory of waking was a fuzzy haze. Had James really made her breakfast? She vaguely remembered his face leaning over her own and the last thing that he whispered to her: "I am ready."

She had been strong and stoic until he left, which was almost immediately. She had waited until she was alone to cry, and when she was alone, she cried hard and deep. She had never cried that hard before. She was surprised by how loud her crying was and how little control she had over it. When she was done, she was exhausted. She ate the breakfast of fruit and a cake because James had left it for her, not because she had desire for food. She could not remember what her breakfast tasted like. She was numb. Apparently she was numb enough to hide it from her sons.

The knock that Bat-Ami dreaded all day never came. One moment she was working at their dinner, and the next moment she turned around and was startled to find both of her sons and both of James' advisers standing in Leander's front room. The look on their faces told her that the four men had already talked. And she knew what they had said.

Knowing she would hear the news of James' death did not prepare her to receive it. The dizziness made her begin to sway, and she found herself being held up by Leander on her left and Bemus on her right.

"Sit here, Mother," Nicholas said as he circled behind her with a wooden chair.

Bat-Ami sat uncomfortably as she looked from one worried male face to another.

Leander appeared at her side again. This time he was holding a rag that he had gotten wet in the rain cask outside of his back door. He held the rag out to her.

"Thank you, Lee," Bat-Ami said as she took the rag. "Please sit down. Everyone, please sit down."

Once all the men were seated, she again became the focal point.

Leander spoke first. "Mother, do you already know what happened to Father today?"

Bat-Ami slowly looked at each face before answering. "I know that James left this morning to go to the Temple and that he knew that he would be asked to betray the Lord Jesus. James knew that he could die if he did not do what they asked."

She watched them. Each man seemed to be holding his breath. Each of them leaned towards her as if wanting her to quicken the telling of her story, but she was speaking as fast as she could. "I know that the last thing James said to me before he left was, 'I am ready.'"

The men broke their circle in response to her last statement. Bemus stood quickly and turned towards the window. Nicholas put his face into his hands. Adrian sat back and, biting his lower lip, watched Leander, who was the only one who held eye contact with her.

"Father knew, then?" asked Leander.

Not knowing, for sure, what had happened that day, she did not know how to answer Leander's question. Bat-Ami moved forward on her chair and faced Adrian. "What happened to James?"

All eyes moved towards Adrian's, while Adrian's own eyes stayed fixed upon Bat-Ami. "I am sorry, Bat-Ami. There is no easy way to say this. What James feared could happen, did happen."

She could feel herself getting dizzy again, but she fought it off. Wiping her face with the rag, she took several deep breaths. When she could talk again, she asked that her sons sit on either side of her. Bemus and Adrian sat across from them.

"Were you at the Temple today?" she asked Adrian and Bemus.

Both men nodded that they were.

"And have you already told my sons what you saw?"

The two men looked at each other.

"They have only told us that Father was..." Nicholas could not finish.

Bat-Ami put her left hand on Nicholas' back as his head lowered.

Adrian interjected, "We only spoke with your sons briefly before Leander suggested that you needed to be part of our conversation."

With her left hand still on Nicholas' back, she turned to see her eldest son watching her through tears pooling in his reddened eyes. She reached out and taking his hand in her right hand she mouthed "thank you." Then, with a hand upon each son, she turned to Adrian and asked, "Would you start from the beginning, please? We need to know everything, even what is hard to say." She felt her right hand being squeezed.

Adrian looked to Bemus, who, by tipping his head towards James' family, invited Adrian to proceed.

"I went to the synagogue very early, and James was already there. He was praying." Adrian looked at Bemus. "Bemus got there shortly after I did. We did not disturb him."

Bemus nodded.

"About midday we walked over to the Temple," continued Adrian.

"How was my father's...mood?" asked Leander.

Adrian hesitated and looked at Bemus, who answered the question. "I would say that he was serious."

"Yes, serious." added Adrian. "When we walk from the synagogue to the Temple, we usually walk slowly and chat and greet people, but we walked much faster today. James seemed very focused. It was as if his mind was already there ahead of us."

Bat-Ami could easily picture her husband in this frame of mind. She had often been with him when his head was already residing where the rest of him was going. She had seen that look many times. It touched her to know that someone else had noticed this about James.

"The Temple courtyard was already crowded when we got there," observed Adrian. "James asked us to stay in the courtyard while he went into the Temple."

"He said he wanted to look Ananus in the eye on his own terms rather than to wait to be summoned," added Bemus.

"That sounds like our father," observed Nicholas. He was the younger of the two sons and the one more likely to invoke his father's discipline. No one on earth knew more about feeling guilty while looking into James' eyes than his younger son, Nicholas.

"It does, Nicholas," agreed Adrian. "Your father always faced his trials head on."

"Excuse me, but earlier I asked if my father knew what he was facing," Leander reminded everyone, "but no one answered me. You are talking like father knew that he was facing danger. Did he?"

Leander watched as Adrian and Bemus both looked at Bat-Ami. Following their eyes, he looked to his mother as well.

"Your father knew that he was going to be asked to speak to the people in the courtyard. He knew that he was going to be asked 'what is the gate unto salvation.' And he knew that the concern was that the people were being 'led astray.'"

"Leading the people astray?" Nicholas asked. "Was that what they said to him?"

"I do not understand what that means," Leander noted as he let go of his mother's hand. "And I do not know who asked him to say these things."

"Ananus," Bat-Ami and Bemus said simultaneously.

Bat-Ami nodded to Bemus, who explained, "The demand upon James to answer that question before the people was most assuredly ordered by Ananus the High Priest. He was under pressure from Herod Agrippa to make a show of strength to the Zealots prior to the new Roman Procurator arriving. We do not know why he chose to use your father this way."

194

Leander shook his head. "I cannot believe that the High Priest thought my father was associated with the Zealots."

"He did not," Nicholas blurted. "No one would have thought that he was a Zealot. It was just an excuse to persecute The Way."

"It is much more likely," explained Bemus, "that this was something personal between James and Ananus. The Sadducees have never had conflict with The Way."

"And that is because of James," added Adrian.

"True," agreed Bemus. "But there has always been tension between James and Ananus."

"Why?" asked Nicholas.

Bemus answered first, "First of all, I want to emphasize that once Ananus was appointed High Priest, James was never anything other than respectful..."

"James was always respectful, even before Ananus became High Priest," interrupted Adrian.

"He reprimanded me just this week for speaking disrespectfully about the High Priest," confessed Bemus. "The tension between them was more related to Ananus' negative feelings towards James than James' feelings towards him."

"Excuse me, please," Bat-Ami interjected softly, "we can go over the history later, if you do not mind. Right now I still want to know what happened to my husband today."

"Yes, of course, Bat-Ami," Bemus apologized. "Forgive me, I am sure that I am avoiding telling this story."

"I can finish, if you would like me to, Bemus," offered Adrian.

Bemus leaned forward and rested his elbows on his knees as he looked down.

"It was shortly after midday when we saw James again. It was the time when the courtyard was most crowded," Adrian began. "I had expected him to speak from the Temple steps, but that is not what

195

happened. The courtyard was as busy and noisy as it usually is during festival times, and then suddenly there was silence. It was eerie."

Bat-Ami folded her arms and sat back in her chair.

"I remember we were all looking at each other, wondering what had happened, and gradually we all noticed that there were two men standing on top of the north tower of the western colonnade. I did not recognize one of them, but the other man was James."

"It was Ananus' nephew, Ronen," offered Bemus.

"The other man, Ronen, spoke first. He introduced James to the crowd as 'the just one, whom we are all bound to obey.'" Adrian sneered. "And then he asked James to explain to the people what the gate unto salvation is so that the people would not be deceived and be led astray."

Nicholas sat upright. "This Ronen person stood him on top of that tower and used those words?"

"What words?" asked Leander.

"The words about leading the people astray, Lee," explained Nicholas. "He brought Father up there because he thought that the threat of being stoned would make Father denounce the Lord Jesus."

Leaner furrowed his brow. "He must not have known Father at all." Looking at his mother he added, "No threat would ever have gotten him to denounce the Lord."

"And it did not," noted Bemus.

"What did Father do?" asked Leander.

Adrian straightened up where he sat. "He was magnificent." And then, looking directly at Bat-Ami, he repeated it. "James was absolutely magnificent, Bat-Ami. James stepped up to the edge and he proclaimed the truth."

"It was…magnificent." emphasized Bemus.

"What did James say?" asked Bat-Ami.

Adrian stood up. "As I said before, James stepped up to the edge—" Adrian took a step forward and extended his arms, reenacting

196

what had happened on the tower—"and he proclaimed, 'Why do you ask me about Jesus, the Son of Man? He is seated now at the right hand of His Father, the Lord our God. And He is coming again on the clouds of heaven."

Bat-Ami reached out and took hold of each of her sons. Adrian had been looking upward rather than downward as he reenacted James' words. Bat-Ami wondered if James had actually been looking into heaven and was describing what he was seeing as he spoke.

As Adrian sat back down, Bemus noted, "Time seemed to stand still. No one in that courtyard spoke or moved."

Again they were all silent. And again it was Bat-Ami who broke the silence. "Please, Adrian, go on."

Adrian looked toward Bemus, who sat unmoving, and then he studied his hands as he wrung them together. After a deep breath, he raised his eyes and swallowed. "I do not know how long it was after James finished speaking. Everything seemed so unreal, but…that other man stepped up behind James and pushed him."

Bat-Ami closed her eyes and held her breath.

"Who pushed him? Ronen?" Nicholas demanded as he stood up.

"Please Nicholas," Bat-Ami said as she reached for his forearm, "sit back down."

As Nicholas sat down sideways on his chair, Bat-Ami glanced at her older son to see how he was. Leander looked pained, but less in need of his mother than her younger son, so she turned back to face Nicholas and took both of his hands in her own.

From behind her, she could hear Leander remark, "So that is how they killed him."

She did not expect a response to Leander's statement; it was simply his way to sum up the end. She was a bit startled to hear Bemus awkwardly clear his throat.

"That is not exactly how James died," said Bemus tentatively.

Nicholas and Leander both sat upright again. Nicholas dislodged his hands from his mother's hands and turned to face Bemus. Bat-Ami simply turned her head.

Bemus shrank back from their stares.

"He did not die in the fall?" asked Leander.

"No, James was still alive after he fell." Bemus' voice cracked, and he buried his face into his hands.

Adrian leaned forward and gently rubbed Bemus' back as he noted, "Bemus was close enough to get to James before he died."

Wiping his face and struggling to breathe, Bemus lifted his face. "There were several of us who got to James immediately. I do not know who else heard it, but," Bemus strained again to breathe, "I saw him lift his head, and I heard him say, 'Father, forgive them, for they know not what they do.'" Bemus could no longer fight off the emotion and began sobbing loudly.

Bat-Ami was not aware of squeezing Leander's hand. Again she held her breath and waited for Bemus to continue. When the sobbing started to slow, she asked softly, "What else did he say, Bemus?"

Seeing that Bemus was still distraught, Adrian answered for his friend, "He does not know, Bat-Ami. Others rushed forward and pushed Bemus away."

Bemus lifted his head and looked at Adrian. The two men stared at each other.

"Please tell us what you are not saying," Bat-Ami begged.

"They stoned him," Adrian said solemnly.

At this, Bat-Ami took her turn to bury her face into her hands and sob. She could feel the hands of her sons on her head and shoulders. She could feel each of them standing on either side of her. The hand on the back of her head was trembling.

It was Leander's voice that she heard ask, "Where is my father's body?"

"We buried him there in the courtyard." answered Adrian.

"It is what he deserved," added Bemus.

Bat-Ami stood up. "Take us to the Temple."

CHAPTER TWENTY-ONE

Where you have envy and selfish ambition,
There you find disorder and every evil practice.
James 3: 16

"How long has it been?" Nathan asked her, as Nicholas brought her back from the cooking portico behind the house.

Bat-Ami did not have to be told that Nathan was referring to the time since James' death. "Four week," she answered, "but it seems like much longer." She extended her palm towards a chair near the front window. "Please, sit," she said as she seated herself along the wall.

Nathan stood next to the chair that he had been offered. "Will you be so kind to join your mother and me, Nicholas? I believe that I have some news that will be of interest to you, too." Then as he sat down Nathan asked, "Leander will be interested too. Is he here?"

"No, he is not. Leander is still working and living at his home beyond the Essene gate. Nicholas is staying with me here until we decide what is to be done with this house."

While Bat-Ami answered Nathan, Nicholas retrieved another chair from the far corner opposite the front window and sat it next to his mother. "Do you have news about the men who murdered my father?"

"Some, but not enough to lay it to rest. The young Sadducee, Ronen, has disappeared from Jerusalem."

"Disappeared?" asked Nicholas. "Do you mean that he fled?"

"I think disappeared is the right term. I do not believe that Ananus knows where his nephew is."

"Do you really think Ananus would hesitate to lie?" Nicholas' question prompted his mother to reach for and hold his hand.

"Ordinarily no, but I do think Ananus would think twice about lying to Beatrice. He could not afford to lose favor with her," Nathan explained. "And it was Beatrice to whom he made the statement."

"Who knows where the coward is then?' Nicholas sneered.

"It is possible that 'the coward' is dead, Nicholas. Mind you, it is only a rumor, and I am not as well skilled at deciphering rumors as James' man Bemus, but I have heard that he is dead."

"Did he die painfully?" asked Nicholas.

"That is enough, Nickie!" declared Bat-Ami, "Nathan is our friend and he is here out of respect for your father. I want to hear what he has to say."

Nicholas turned slightly to face Nathan squarely, "You were my father's trusted friend. He spoke of you with respect and affection and with that knowledge I also hold you in high regard. Please accept my apology if my…eagerness for justice has offended you."

"No apology is necessary, Nicholas. I understand perfectly. I, too, am anxious for justice. Your father was, no let me rephrase that, your father *is* one of the men that I respect the most. I am impatient for justice. But I do appreciate your apology, and if you do not mind my noting, you sounded very much like your father just then."

Nicholas' shoulders dropped slightly and in a deeper slower voice, he said, "Thank you."

Bat-Ami smiled at the comparison too.

"If the rumor that has come to me is true," Nathan continued, "then Ronen died quickly and violently in the desert. One story is that his throat was slit and the other story is that he was dragged behind a horse into the En-Gedi."

Bat-Ami shuddered and closed her eyes. "Who would do this, Nathan? It is hardly what James would have approved of."

"I do not know, Bat-Ami, I am sorry. But one possibility is that the murder of Ronen was done by the same man who led the stoning of James in the courtyard. It may be that…"

Bat-Ami placed her face in her hands and wept while Nicholas placed his right hand gently on the back of her head.

Nathan waited while Bat-Ami composed herself, and when she finally looked up he said, "I am sorry. I should have chosen my words more cautiously."

"It is not your fault, Nathan. We do want to hear everything that you have come to share with us," Bat-Ami said, trying to comfort him. "It is still a very fresh wound. We are fine." She looked toward Nicholas. "Aren't we, Nickie?"

"We are in the season of grieving and it is hard, but we do not expect it to be otherwise," Nicholas agreed. "Can you explain why the man who…stoned my father would also murder the man who pushed him from the top of the Temple?"

"Again, it is only rumor, but the story is that whoever it was that did that to James was lied to about whom he was stoning. If that is true, then it is easy to imagine him being outraged and turning his violence on whomever lied to him."

Nicholas looked at his mother. "I know that it is wrong to feel this way, but it does seem just to me, Mother."

Bat-Ami smiled patiently at her son and then looked to Nathan. "Thank you, Nathan for coming here to keep us informed. It is very kind of you."

Nathan scooted forward in his seat. "You are welcome. It is the least that I could do, but none of that was what I came here to tell you about."

Bat-Ami looked startled. "It isn't?"

"No, it is not. I was just responding to your question," Nathan said sheepishly. "I really came here to tell you about Ananus."

Mentioning Ananus made Bat-Ami's and Nicholas' to scoot forward in their chairs.

Nathan leaned back and held up his palms. "I have something to tell you, and I wanted you to hear it first, but you must promise me that you will speak of it to no one until after it happens."

"Until after what happens?" asked Nicholas.

"What about Leander, my other son?" asked Bat-Ami simultaneously.

Nathan pointed to Bat-Ami first. "If you can get him to promise secrecy first, then you have my permission to tell him. But—" he turned his finger towards Nicholas— "I must have your word that you will keep what I am about to tell you to yourselves at least until after it becomes public knowledge." He put his finger down and took a deep breath. "It should only be a day or two at the most that your silence will be required."

Bat-Ami looked at her son and they nodded at each other. "We agree," she said.

"About a week ago," began Nathan, "a group of Pharisees had an audience with Felix, the Roman Governor in Galilee. A Shammi named Nathaniel, who wanted to make sure that Felix was fully informed about the state of Jerusalem politics, led the delegation. And James' death was, as Nathaniel suspected, a surprise to Felix."

"Did the Governor know my father?" asked Nicholas.

"He did not know James personally, but he knew James' reputation. And he was quite distressed to hear of James' death. Nathaniel told Felix that James was executed."

Bat-Ami and Nicholas both flinched.

"It was clever of Nathaniel to describe it as an execution because, as you know, the Romans do not allow anyone else to engage in

203

capital punishment. And it worked because Felix told the delegation that he would take it up with Herod Agrippa himself."

Nathan took a moment to breathe and stretch. Either Bat-Ami or Nicholas could have used the open moment to ask a question or make a comment, but neither did. They both waited patiently for Nathan to continue.

"Agrippa and Beatrice met with Felix in Joppa yesterday, and it was ugly. Felix was not angry, and he made himself perfectly clear. Agrippa is to establish order and control or Rome would find someone else who would. Herod Agrippa tried to save face as best as he could. He made excuses. I was embarrassed for him. And Beatrice, she tried to disappear. I have never seen her speechless, but she had nothing to say in Joppa or on the way back to Jerusalem. Agrippa was furious."

"What is to happen, Nathan?" asked Bat-Ami.

Nathan's smiled proudly. "Tomorrow, Herod Agrippa will summon Ananus the High Priest to the Palace. Ananus does not know it yet, and that is why I must remind you of your pledge of secrecy, but his days as High Priest are over."

CHAPTER TWENTY-TWO

Anyone, then, who knows
The good he ought to do
And doesn't do it, sins.
James 4: 17

"**A**nanus will be told tomorrow!" Leander repeated gleefully as he finished the last of the flatbread. The earlier conversation between Nathan, Nicholas, and Bat-Ami had been hurriedly recounted to Leander when he arrived home for their evening meal, and then it was retold more slowly after Nicholas finished offering the blessing for it.

"It is not enough," Nicholas added, "but it is at least something."

"Yes, and it is interesting that it was the Pharisees who sought justice," Leander noted.

"I do not know if they were seeking justice or simply availing themselves of the opportunity to strike a blow against Ananus for their own purposes," countered Nicholas.

Bat-Ami glanced at her younger son out of the corner of her eye. *You, my son, are becoming both astute and cynical. Be careful.*

A more serious look crossed Leander's face as he tightened his eyelids and seemed to stare at nothing in particular on the table. "Did either of you get the impression from your conversation with Nathan that Father knew what was going to happen to him when he went to Temple that day?"

"That is the question that you asked Adrian and Bemus a month ago, is it not?" Nicholas asked Leander.

205

Stroking the back of her son's hand as it rested on the table, Bat-Ami asked, "You know that he was ready, don't you, Lee?"

"I do, Mother." Leander looked at his mother through watery eyes. "But being ready for it if it happens and being sure that it will happen are quite different," as he wiped his cheek. "I do not suppose that is a question anyone can answer, but it is the question I keep asking myself."

"Why, Lee?" Bat-Ami asked softly. "Why isn't knowing that he was prepared and ready enough? Why are you tormenting yourself?"

"Because," Leander said as he removed his hand from underneath his mother's hand. He paused to look into each of their eyes before confessing, "I keep wondering if I would have had Father's courage if that task had fallen to me." He folded his arms across the table before him and rested his forehead upon them.

Bat-Ami watched her son's body tremble but heard no sound from him. She stood next to him and leaned her hip against his side, stroking the back of his head. As he stilled, she leaned down and spoke into his ear, assuring him. "If the Lord called you to such a task, Lee, then the Lord would equip you to see it through. You need not compare yourself to any man other than the man God our Father created you to be."

Leander sat up and put his hand on top of his mother's hand, which was now resting on his shoulder. "You sounded just like Father."

She smiled. "I should sound like James. I have listened to him for many, many years."

"Lee," Nicholas said from across the table, "I have been thinking about your question, too. Do you remember that last conversation we had with Father?"

Leander nodded.

"I have recounted that conversation over and over in my mind."

"I have as well," agreed Leander.

"I think he said good-bye to us that night."

Bat-Ami returned to her chair. "What did he say, Nickie?"

Nicholas looked at his older brother and offered him the opportunity to answer their mother's question.

"We laughed about your hiding parsnip roots in his food," Leander said to Bat-Ami, who just smiled. "And then he told us about feeling pressure from people who wanted his life to be as extraordinary as they thought it should be."

"That is right," Nicholas blurted, "Father said 'people who look for the unusual miss how extraordinary the ordinary really is.'"

Leander waited for his brother's excitement to calm before continuing, "He told a story about being asked about his father."

"Do you mean Joseph?" Bat-Ami asked.

"Yes. Father said that he was crossing Jerusalem once and a man walking along beside him asked Father what Joseph felt like not being Jesus' father."

"What a strange question," observed Bat-Ami. "What did James say to that?"

"He said that 'Joseph never considered that Jesus was not his son.' He said, 'Sons are a heritage from the Lord, no matter how the Lord gives them.'"

"And...," Nicholas prodded.

Leander sent a look of irritation towards his younger brother, "And then he said that he felt like his father..."

"Father said he had been blessed by the Lord with Lee and me as his sons," Nicholas impatiently finished. "He offered us that blessing. He said he was proud of his son, Leander, the bear, who was slow and steady and could always be counted on to be thorough and stable and strong."

"Father did not say 'slow,' Nicholas." Turning towards Bat-Ami he said, "And of his younger son, the hawk, he said he was proud of Nick's ability to see small details and to act quickly and decisively."

207

Turning back to Nicholas he added, "But what he really meant was rash and impetuous."

"Snail," Nicholas called his brother.

"A snail is a noble creature, Nicholas," Bat-Ami tried to say with a straight face, but it was no use.

Leander and Nicholas looked at each other across the table and laughed.

"It is good to hear laughter again," Bat-Ami said as she folded her hands and placed them in her lap. "You know, what James said to you sounds very much like a blessing to me."

"It certainly was, Mother," responded Leander as he became more serious. "I think we both realize that."

"Does that not answer your question, Lee?" Bat-Ami asked.

"Do you mean about whether Father knew what was going to happen?" clarified Leander.

Bat-Ami nodded yes, and Leander continued, "Not really, Mother."

"Not really!" she started. "How can you say that, Lee? He made a point of telling you both that he was proud of you. James told me so."

"But Mother," Leander pleaded with his palms extended to either side, "he told us that he was proud of us many times. This time was not so different." Then to Nicholas, "Was it, Nick?"

Nicholas leaned forward, with his arms against the edge of the table. "But it was different, Lee. Do you remember that story he told us from Judges?"

Leander looked confused. "Do you mean that story about the tribe of Benjamin?"

"Yes," answered Nicholas, and then to his mother he explained, "Father often told us stories from the Torah and from the histories of our people."

"He was always teaching," added Leander.

"This story was no different. He said that it was about grace. The Lord our God showed grace upon the tribe of Benjamin after the other tribes nearly destroyed them. Some men of the tribe of Benjamin violated the concubine of a traveling Levite who was staying among them. She died, and when the Levite returned home, he sent her remains in pieces to the other tribes and pleaded for justice." Nicholas paused and took a drink of water. "The other tribes of Israel rose up against Benjamin and would have killed them all if five hundred of them had not run away and hidden in the hills."

"I believe that it was six hundred, not five hundred," Leander corrected his brother.

"That is right, it was six hundred. And after a time all of God's people began to mourn the loss of a tribe of Israel, for although there were still *six* hundred men of Benjamin left, there were no women. And that was a problem because the other tribes had taken an oath not to let their daughters marry the men of Benjamin. So the people cried out to the Lord for the missing tribe. And the Lord had pity on Benjamin and provided women for them so that they might produce heirs and survive."

"I remember that," Leander said excitedly. "Father said that it showed the Lord's grace. The surviving men of Benjamin were told that they could kidnap virgin girls of Shiloh when the girls came out to dance in the fields. But I do not understand how that answers my question."

"You do not remember what father said after that?"

Leander shook his head.

Nicholas sat up straighter. "Father said, 'Remember, my sons, the Lord is always gracious. Sometimes you receive his grade when you do not deserve it, like the tribe of Benjamin. And sometimes—'" Nicholas deepened his voice— "'you are the instrument of his grace, like the dancing girls of Shiloh.'"

CHAPTER TWENTY-THREE

Elijah was a man just like us
He prayed that it would not rain,
and it did not rain on the land
for three and a half years.
James 5:17

B at-Ami stood in the doorway of the home that she had shared
with James for the last two decades and gazed at the empty
front room. It was now six months since she had lost James.
Nicholas would soon be returning to the synagogue in Lydda, and Bat-
Ami was set to move in with Leander. She ran her fingertips across the
mezuzah and remembered James reciting the *shma* as he came and
went.

She felt a hand on her left shoulder. "Are you ready, Bat-Ami?"
Jude asked.

Her brother-in-law and childhood friend, Jude, had joined them
yesterday, and spent the night with them at Leander's home.

"We need to keep walking," Jude reminded her, "but we can stop
here again on the way back from Bezetha if you want."

Bat-Ami and Jude were walking across Jerusalem to attend a
ceremony in Bezetha. The Jerusalem Council had waited nearly half a
year before honoring James' desire to have Symeon named to be his
successor as Bishop of Jerusalem. This day would be Symeon's last as
the Rabbi in the Bezetha synagogue. James' family, including his
brother, Jude, was invited to attend a time of worship, followed by a

banquet in Symeon's honor. Symeon had insisted that they be included. Leander and Nicholas were delivering a cabinet Leander had just finished making and would meet Bat-Ami and their Uncle Jude in Bezetha.

Bat kissed the *mezuzah* for the last time, after receiving the *shma*, turned to Jude, "I am ready."

They walked for a while before Jude broke the silence. "I read the papers that you gave me last night."

"James' epistle?"

"Yes. It made me weep because I could see him saying so much of it." Catching himself, Jude rephrased his words. "Actually I *have* heard him say so much of it."

Bat-Ami nodded. "Me too."

"It is powerful. No one else could say so much with so few words."

"Do you really think so, Jude?" She hesitated, "I want it to get into the hands of the Council, but I was afraid."

"Afraid? Afraid of what?"

"I am a woman, Jude. I am not supposed to be able to read. I know that does not matter to you, but I cannot be the one to bring this forward."

Jude smiled at the mention of their childhood reading lessons. "You know, my mother always said that I might not have ever learned to read if I had not also been trying to teach you."

The mention of Mary brought a smile to Bat-Ami's face. "But you do think that it is good enough to give it to the scribes?"

"I do, don't you?" Jude asked.

"Of course, but I am hardly capable of objectivity. He is my husband...and...it was my idea," Bat-Ami confessed.

"What do you mean, it was your idea?" Jude asked in a startled high pitch.

"You know James, he would never presume to write something and turn it over to the scribes," she explained. "So I collected the notes that

211

he wrote in preparation for sermons." Looking at Jude she added, "He did not know that I was doing it."

Jude grinned. "James did not know?"

"No, but I did tell him eventually. I tried to convince him to leave Jerusalem and go somewhere simpler. I thought that he could write. He had such wisdom to share."

"This is a good thing that you did, Bat-Ami. I believe that this can be a blessing to many." He guided them around a puddle in the walkway. "I wonder what it would have been like if James had known he was writing for others to read. He might have been a little more long-winded."

"James did know about the first part."

"The first part?" asked Jude.

"What I collected were the nine essays. I showed James the essays before I got him to promise to write that whole first part. James knew that he was writing to the twelve tribes when he wrote that. I think it might be the first five pages in the stack that I gave you."

Jude scratched his upper lip. "Now that you mention it, I thought those five pages seemed newer. They were not weathered or faded."

"Those pages are newer," Bat-Ami confirmed. "I had been saving some of those other pages for over two years."

"That means that I was wrong about him being more long-winded if he knew that he was writing to be read. The essays, as you called them, were short enough, but those first five pages were very brief. It was more like a list or even an eruption of things that he wanted to say in a hurry. Maybe knowing he was leaving a written piece for all of us made him nervous enough to be even more concise than more long-winded."

"You know James well, Jude. If he had known, and if he had had more time, I believe he would have been more long-winded."

"What are you saying, Bat?"

Bat-Ami stopped walking and turned to face Jude. "He wrote those five pages the night before he died, Jude. He had no more time."

"And he knew that?" asked Jude solemnly.

"He knew that."

Jude swallowed hard and looked away.

"Those are his last words to the twelve tribes. He knew that Luke and Paul and John and Peter were writing. James wrote what he wanted to make sure that the people of God would know, but that Peter and Paul would not write."

"It is a guide to maturing in faith," Jude summed up James' writing.

"It is," Bat-Ami agreed. "It is."

The banquet for Symeon was a simple but joyous affair held in a home near Symeon's home where the synagogue met to worship. The front room would hardly have contained the sixty people who had gathered in the back terrace to celebrate Rabbi Symeon's appointment to become the Rabbi at James' synagogue. Bat-Ami was given a seat of honor underneath an overhead trellis that had held grapevines through the summer. It was the most shaded and pleasant place for her to sit. She watched Jude and Nicholas in one corner of the terrace engage in what looked like a lively conversation with several older men. Bat-Ami assumed that these were the elders and the conversation was a debate about some minor theological point that men liked to quibble over.

Bat-Ami watched as the guests came and went from inside the house where the banquet table held an array of cakes, fruit, and meats. The sound of lively conversation and light laughter was everywhere. Leander made several trips inside, obviously enjoying the food more than the conversation with his uncle and brother. Bat-Ami could not help but see that several young women had noticed her eldest son.

Bishop Symeon and his wife, Isaura, stood near the back door to the house, where they spoke to the individual guests as each came by to express congratulations or appreciation. Isaura seemed rather frail when she was introduced earlier, but now she appeared more at east. Graciousness befit her. It was clear that the people of Bezetha loved them both. Bat-Ami was pleased, because by tomorrow it would be Symeon and Isaura that would occupy the home where she and James had raised their family. She knew that James would have been pleased, too.

Bat-Ami's thoughts wandered to the worship service, which consisted of prayers for the people of Bezetha, Jerusalem, Judea, and Israel, the singing of psalms, and a teaching by Symeon. For his lesson, Symeon chose the prayer life of Elijah. He was not an eloquent orator, but Bat-Ami was impressed with his lesson. There was no question about his earnestness. He spoke of Elijah's faith: "In faith Elijah fearlessly confronted the evil King Ahab. In faith Elijah waited while the ravens fed him manna. In faith Elijah confronted the priests of Baal on Mount Carmel. And in spite of Elijah's belief that God his Father had forsaken him, in faith he crossed the desert in forty days and on Mount Horeb he received a new call."

As they walked to the banquet, Jude had said, "I wonder if the young Rabbi considers the journey from Bezetha to Jerusalem to be like Elijah's journey through the desert?"

James would have thought so, she had thought to herself.

Bat-Ami was startled out of her pleasant thoughts as she felt something being placed in her hands, which were folded in her lap.

"I am so sorry to startle you," said a woman that Bat-Ami did not recognize. "You are James' wife, are you not?"

Bat-Ami lifted her hand and looked at the pale blue wildflower she held. "I am."

The woman was middle-aged, with dark hair and eyes. She introduced herself as Mary. The only distinguishing characteristic about her was the unusual shawl that she gathered around her shoulders. It was still too warm for a shawl, and it was certainly too warm for a shawl that was as dark as this one. It was the darkest shawl Bat had ever seen, and it seemed to sparkle as if it had flecks of gold woven in the fabric.

The woman leaned close and softly said, "I did not know your husband for very long, but I wanted to tell you how much I appreciated him." She reached out and gently squeezed Bat-Ami's left hand. "He always carried himself with such confidence. It was like…like…I don't know." Mary looked embarrassed as she gritted her teeth and squeezed Bat-Ami's hand once more.

Placing her right hand on top of Mary's hand Bat-Ami helped finish her thought. "James did carry himself with confidence. I think it was because he knew exactly who he was."

EPILOGUE

James, Peter, and John, those reputed to be pillars
gave me and Barnabas the right hand of fellowship
when they recognized the grace given to me.
They agreed that we should go to the Gentiles,
and they to the Jews.
Galatians 2:9

Four years after James' death, in 66 AD, his brother Jude wrote his epistle. Jude's urge for the people of God to "contend for the faith" may have been inspired by his brother's uncompromising contention for the faith. His courage to write at all and his use of the term "pollute" may demonstrate the influence of his childhood friend and sister-in-law.

In 70 AD, eight years after James' death, Jerusalem was destroyed by the Romans. The Romans did not want to destroy Jerusalem, but skirmishes with the Zealots became progressively worse and something had to be done. The Zealot uprising had retreated to the Temple for a last stand. The other sects in Jerusalem did not want to fight the Romans, but they could not tolerate the Romans attacking the Temple.

When it was over, Jerusalem was devastated and the Temple destroyed. The Zealots were crushed, the Sadducees were obliterated, and the Herodians were displaced. The Pharisees survived because selective members of their sect were willing to bargain with the Romans for safe passage out of the siege in return for not resisting. It was not until 70 AD that Symeon was named the second Bishop of Jerusalem.

Bat-Ami, Leander, Nicholas, and other members of James' family would likely have fled Jerusalem to escape annihilation. After fleeing Roman-occupied Israel, they may have traveled as far away as they could. Using Roman means of transportation, but running from Roman rule, they could have traveled as far west as Britain, the western edge of the Roman Empire. From Britain they could have turned north and traveled far enough to be beyond Roman reach. That would have been Scotland. It is possible that they chose for themselves a family name that honored their patriarch, James. James had called himself a "servant of God and the Lord Jesus the Messiah." It would be fitting for Bat-Ami and her sons and grandchildren to have chosen the name servant, which in Scotland would have been Steward.

Is it not an odd coincidence that a Scottish family of servants would eventually produce a line of Kings that would span six generations? Is it not an odd coincidence that when the Steward or Stewart family produced men, they became Kings and were all named James? Is it not an odd coincidence that the sixth James Stewart, King of Scotland, also became James Stewart the First, King of England, who commissioned the most widely read English language translation of the Scriptures? Is it not an odd coincidence that he named that translation the King *James?* Is it just an odd coincidence...or is it something else? We do not know.

Sources and Suggested Readings

The Acts of the Apostles, Revised Edition.
William Barclay.
Philadephia: Westminster Press, 1976.
ISBN: 0-664-21306-5
Pbk: 0-664-24106-9

Anchor Bible Dictionary. Vol III; V
David Noel Freedman, editor in chief.
New York: Doubleday, 1992.

Ancient Israel: From Abraham to the Roman Destruction of the Temple.
Edited by Hershel Shanks.
Biblical Archaeology Society, 1999.
ISBN: 1-880317-54-0

Bandits, Prophets, and Messiahs: Popular Movements in the Time of Jesus.
Richard A. Horsley with John S. Hanson.
San Francisco: Harper & Row, Publishers, 1988.
ISBN: 0-86683-993-3

The Birth of Christianity; The First Twenty Years.
After Jesus, Vol. I.
Paul Barnett.

Grand Rapids: Wm. B. Eerdmans Publishing Co., 2005.
ISBN-10: 0-8028-2781-0
Or ISBN-13: 978-0-8028-2781-4

Daily Life in Ancient Israel.
Essays and Catalog of an Exhibition at the Yeshiva University Museum,
November 1980-June 1981.
By Harold Liebowitz (Guest Curator)
1980
ISBN: N/A
Same title located on Amazon listed the following: ASIN: B0006E5MBC
Daily Life in Biblical Times.
Oded Borowski.
Society of Biblical Literature, 2003.
ISBN: 1-58983-042-3

The First Jewish Revolt: Archaeology, history, and ideology.
Edited by Andrea M. Berlin & J. Andrew Overman.
Routledge-Taylor and Francis Group, 2002.
ISBN: 0-415-25706-9

Flavius Josephus: Eyewitnesses to Rome's First Century Conquest of Judea.
Mireille Hadas-Lebel; translated by Richard Miller.
Macmillan Publishing Co., 1993.
ISBN: 0-02-547161-9

In the Shadow of the Temple; Jewish Influences on Early Christianity.
Oskar Skarsaune.

Intervarsity Press, 2002.
ISBN: 0-8308-2760-X.

Israel in Revolution: 6-74 C.E.: A Political History Based on the Writings of Josephus.
David M. Rhoads.
Fortress Press, 1976.
ISBN: 0-8006-0442-3

Jewish New Testament.
Translated by David H. Stern.
Jewish New Testament Publications, Inc., 1989.
ISBN: 965-359-003-0

Power and Politics in Palestine: The Jews and the Governing of their Land 100 BC-AD 70.
James S. McLaren.
Sheffield Academic Press, 1991.
ISBN: 1-85075-319-9

The Ruling Class of Judea: The Origins of the Jewish Revolt Against Rome A.D. 66-70.
Martin Goodman.
Cambridge University Press, 1987.
ISBN: 0-521-33401-2

Talk Thru the New Testament.
Talk Thru the Bible Vol. II.
Bruce Wilkinson and Kenneth Boa.
Thomas Nelson Publishers, 1983.
ISBN: 0-8407-5286-5 (Nelson)
ISBN: 0-8407-5353-5 (set)

The Works of Flavius Josephus. Vol. I-IV.
William Whitson, A.M.
Grand Rapids: Baker Book House, 1974.
ISBN: 0-8010-5056-1
Vol. 1: The Wars of the Jews
Vol. 2: The Life of Flavius Josephus: Antiquities of the Jews; I-VIII
Vol. 3: Antiquities of the Jews; IX-XVII
Vol. 4: Antiquities of the Jews; XVIII-XX; Flavius Josephus Against Apion; Concerning Hades; Appendix; Index

About the Author

CHUCK THOMPSON is an Associate Professor of Psychology and Religion at King College, where he is also the Director of the Counseling Center serving both the campus and the community. "Over the past ten years, I have come to organize more and more of my counseling style and technique around the first chapter of the Epistle of James," Chuck says. "This chapter is the most comprehensive list of spiritual formation and personal growth concerns ever written. It has highly influenced how I engage in the people-helping field."

A college class he has taught for the past seven years is formed around his two books on the personal application of James: *The James*

Prescription and *Slipping and Sliding Through Trials* (James One Institute). Another title, *Presence and Truth* (James One Institute), applies this same material to the art of counseling (Chuck has taught an additional college course on Christian counseling for the past two years). Currently he is rewriting *The James Prescription* and another novel based on Elijah the Prophet.

For more information on Chuck Thompson:

www.jamesoneinstitute.com

Other Books by Chuck Thompson

Soon to be available at www.amazon.com
All books are available at www.jamesoneinstitute.com

The James Prescription, an applied theology book, is based upon the first chapter of the Epistle of James. Wisdom begins as the key essentials of a trial are noticed and proceeds as the trial and solution are both named effectively. James' first chapter is a survey of what to notice in order to face trials of many kinds with joy and wisdom.

Slipping and Sliding Through Trials is a sequel to *The James Prescription,* but instead of focusing on the trials we face, it focuses on the pollutions we have acquired in the past. It is a survey of what to notice in order to rid ourselves of the pollutants from past experiences.

Presence and Truth: Christian Existential Counseling offers a basic strategy for counseling others that is true to orthodox Christian faith, is effective, is simple, and is flexible enough to incorporate other counseling theories and techniques. Thompson asserts that the twin elements of Presence and Truth telling are the requirements for one person to have a therapeutic impact upon another. For "truth-telling" he directs us to be mindful of the wisdom found within the first chapter of James.

From Mount Carmel to Mount Horeb: Elijah's Journey through Depression looks at the life of the prophet Elijah as an example of reactive depression. Thompson's view of the redemptive possibilities within the trials of Elijah is evidenced by his explanation of how God worked to transform Elijah from the fearless challenger of Ahab the King to the founder of the school of prophets and the mentor of Elisha, his successor.

www.ingramcontent.com/pod-product-compliance
Lightning Source LLC
Chambersburg PA
CBHW070617130626
46556CB00001B/393